"How would you feel if a bear made its den beside this stream?"

Cole shrugged. "I'd kill it."

The potbellied elder nodded with a knowing smile. "Animals feel the same way. Don't forget that. You aren't the only creature here. You're part of a much bigger circle. Learn your place or you'll have a rough time."

"What is there to learn?"

"Patience, gentleness, strength, honesty. Animals can teach us more about ourselves than any teacher." He stared away toward the south. "Off the coast of British Columbia, there is a special black bear called the Spirit Bear. It's pure white and has pride, dignity, and honor. More than most people."

"If I saw a Spirit Bear, I'd kill it," Cole said.

Edwin tightened his grip on Cole as if in warning. "Whatever you do to the animals, you do to yourself. Remember that."

Books by Ben Mikaelsen

TOUCHING SPIRIT BEAR
Winner:

North Dakota Flicker Tale Book Award
Nautilus Award for Young Adult Literature
California Young Reader Medal
Nevada Young Readers' Award

Nominee:

Kansas Heartland Award
Texas Lone Star Reading List
Utah Young Adults' Book Award
New Mexico Land of Enchantment Book Award
Western Writers of America Golden Spur Award Finalist
Sequoyah Young Adult Book Award (Oklahoma)
Rebecca Caudill Young Reader's Book Award
(Illinois)
Young Hoosier Book Award (Indiana)
South Carolina Young Adult Book Award
Arizona Young Readers Award
Wyoming Soaring Eagle Book Award
Pacific Northwest Library Association Reader's Choice
Award
Maude Hart Lovelace Book Award (Minnesota)
Kentucky Bluegrass Award

TOUCHING
SPIRIT
BEAR

BEN MIKAELSEN

HarperTrophy®
An imprint of HarperCollins Publishers

Harper Trophy® is a registered trademark of HarperCollins Publishers Inc.

Touching Spirit Bear
Copyright © 2001 by Ben Mikaelsen

Library of Congress Cataloging-in-Publication Data
Mikaelsen, Ben, 1952–
Touching Spirit Bear / by Ben Mikaelsen.
p.   cm.
Summary: After his anger erupts into violence, Cole, in order to avoid going to prison,
agrees to participate in a sentencing alternative based on the Native American Circle
Justice, and he is sent to a remote Alaskan island where an encounter with a huge Spirit
Bear changes his life.
ISBN 0-380-97744-3 — ISBN 0-06-029149-4 (lib. bdg.)
ISBN 0-380-80560-X (pbk.) — ISBN 0-06-073400-0 (pbk.)
[1. Juvenile delinquents—Rehabilitation—Fiction. 2. Anger—Fiction.
3. Forgiveness—Fiction. 4. Child abuse—Fiction. 5. Tlingit Indians—Fiction.
6. Indians of North America—Alaska—Fiction.] I. Title.
PZ7.M5926 To 2000   00-040702
[Fic]—dc21   CIP
                                                                        AC

❖

First Harper Trophy edition, 2002
First rack edition, 2005
Visit us on the World Wide Web!
www.harperteen.com

ACKNOWLEDGMENT

A special thanks to those who patiently helped me understand the healing ways of Circle Justice.

DEDICATION

This book is dedicated to Buffy,
a seven-hundred-pound black bear who
has become my own Spirit Bear.
He taught me to be gentle and
that I, too, am part of
the Circle.

Fall seven times, stand up eight.
—JAPANESE PROVERB

Part One

TOUCHING
SPIRIT
BEAR

CHAPTER 1

C OLE MATTHEWS KNELT defiantly in the bow of the aluminum skiff as he faced forward into a cold September wind. Worn steel handcuffs bit at his wrists each time the small craft slapped into another wave. Overhead, a gray-matted sky hung like a bad omen. Cole strained at the cuffs even though he had agreed to wear them until he was freed on the island to begin his banishment. Agreeing to spend a whole year alone in Southeast Alaska had been his only way of avoiding a jail cell in Minneapolis.

Two men accompanied Cole on this final leg of his journey. In the middle sat Garvey, the gravelly-voiced, wisecracking Indian parole officer from Minneapolis. Garvey said he was a Tlingit Indian, pronouncing *Tlingit* proudly with a click-ing of his tongue as if saying "Klingkit." He was built like a bulldog with lazy eyes. Cole didn't trust Garvey. He didn't trust anyone who wasn't afraid of him. Garvey pretended to be a friend, but Cole knew he was nothing more than a paid baby-sitter. This week his job was escorting a violent juvenile offender first from Minneapolis to Seattle, then to Ketchikan, Alaska, where they boarded a big silver floatplane to the Tlingit village of Drake. Now they were headed for some island in the middle of nowhere.

In the rear of the skiff sat Edwin, a quiet, potbellied Tlingit elder who had helped arrange Cole's banishment. He steered the boat casually, a faded blue T-shirt and baggy jeans his only protection against the wind. Deep-set eyes made it hard to tell what Edwin was thinking. He stared forward with a steely patience, like a wolf waiting. Cole didn't trust him either.

It was Edwin who had built the shelter and made all the preparations on the island where Cole was to stay. When he first met Edwin in Drake, the gruff elder took one look and pointed a finger at him. "Go put your clothes on inside out," he ordered.

"Get real, old man," Cole answered.

"You'll wear them reversed for the first two weeks of your banishment to show humility and shame," Edwin said, his voice hard as stone. Then he turned and shuffled up the dock toward his old rusty pickup.

Cole hesitated, eyeing the departing elder.

"Just do it," Garvey warned.

Still standing on the dock in front of everyone, Cole smirked as he undressed. He refused to turn his back as he slowly pulled each piece inside out—even his underwear. Villagers watched from the shore until he finished changing.

Bracing himself now against the heavy seas, Cole held that same smirk. His blue jeans, heavy wool shirt, and rain jacket chafed his skin, but it didn't matter. He would have worn a cowbell around his neck if it had meant avoiding jail. He wasn't a Tlingit Indian. He was an innocent-looking, baby-faced fifteen-year-old from Minneapolis who had been in trouble with the law half his life. Everyone thought he felt sorry for what he had done, and going to this island was his way of making things right.

Nothing could be further from the truth. To Cole, this was just another big game. With salt air biting at his face, he turned and glanced at Edwin. The elder eyed him back with a dull stare. Anger welled up inside Cole. He hated that stupid stare. Pretending to aim toward the waves, he spit so the wind would catch the thick saliva and carry it back.

The spit caught Edwin squarely and dragged across his faded shirt. Edwin casually lifted an oily rag from the bottom of the skiff and wiped away the slime, then tossed the rag back under his seat and again fixed his eyes on Cole.

Cole feigned surprise as if he had made a horrible mistake, then twisted at the handcuffs again. What was this old guy's problem anyway? The elder acted fearless, but he had to be afraid of something. Everyone in the world was afraid of something.

Cole thought back to all the people at home who had tried to help him over the years. He hated their fake concern. They didn't really care what happened to him. They were gutless—he could see it in their eyes. They were afraid, glad to be rid of him. They pretended to help only because they didn't know what else to do.

For years, "help" had meant sending him to drug counseling and anger therapy sessions. Every few months, Cole found himself being referred to someone else. He discovered early on that "being referred" was the adult term for passing the buck. Already he had seen the inside of a dozen police stations, been through as many counselors, a psychologist, several detention centers, and two residential treatment centers.

Each time he got into trouble, he was warned to shape up because this was his last chance. Even the day he left for the island, several of those who gathered to see him off, including his parents, had warned him, "Don't screw up. This is your last chance." Cole braced himself for the next big wave. Whatever happened, he could always count on having one more *last* chance.

Not that it really mattered. He had no intention of ever honoring the contract he agreed to during the Circle Justice meetings. As soon as they left him alone, this silly game would end. Circle Justice was a bunch of bull. They were crazy if they thought he was going to spend a whole year of his life like some animal, trapped on a remote Alaskan island.

Cole twisted at the handcuffs again. Last year at this time, he had never even heard of Circle Justice—he hadn't heard of it until his latest arrest for breaking into a hardware store. After robbing the place, he had totally trashed it.

The police might not have caught him, but after a week passed, he bragged about the break-in at school. When someone ratted on him, the police questioned Cole. He denied the break-in, of course, and then he beat up the boy who had turned him in.

The kid, Peter Driscal, was a ninth grader Cole had picked on many times before just for the fun of it. Still, no one ratted on Cole Matthews without paying the price. That day, he caught up to Peter in the hallway at school. "You're a dead man," he warned the skinny red-haired boy, giving him a hard shove. He laughed when he saw fear in Peter's eyes.

Later, after school, Cole cornered Peter outside in the parking lot. With anger that had been brewing all day, he attacked him and started hitting him hard in the face with his bare fists. Peter was no match, and soon Cole had pounded him bloody. A dozen students stood watching. When Peter tried to escape, he tripped and fell to the ground. Cole jumped on him again and started smashing his head against the sidewalk. It took six other students to finally pull him away. By then Peter was cowering on the blood-smeared sidewalk, sobbing. Cole laughed and spit at him even as he was held back. Nobody crossed Cole Matthews and got away with it.

Because of his vicious attack on Peter Driscal, Cole had been kept at a detention center while the courts decided what to do with him. His white-walled room was bare except for a bed with a gray blanket, a toilet without a cover, a shelf for clothes, a cement table, and a barred window facing onto the center group area. The place smelled like cleaning disinfectant.

Each night guards locked the room's thick steel door. They called this detention space a room, but Cole knew it was really a jail cell. A room didn't need a locked steel door. During the day, guards allowed Cole to go into the central group area with other juveniles if he wanted to. He could read, watch TV, or talk. They expected him to do schoolwork with a tutor that came each day. What a joke. This was no school, and he was no student. Cole did as little as absolutely possible, keeping to himself. The other detainees were a bunch of losers.

Cole figured he wouldn't even be here if Peter Driscal had known how to fight back. Instead, Peter was hospitalized. Doctors' reports warned he might suffer permanent damage. "Serves him right," Cole mumbled when he was first told of Peter's condition.

What angered Cole most after this latest arrest were his parents. In the past they had always come running with a lawyer, offering to pay damages and demanding his release. They had enough money and connections to move mountains. Besides, they had a reputation to protect. What parent wanted the world to know their son was a juvenile delinquent? All Cole did was pretend he was sorry for a few days till things blew over. But that was how it had been in the past, before his parents got divorced.

This time, he hadn't been freed. He was told that because of his past record and the violence of this attack, he would be kept locked up while prosecutors filed a motion to transfer him to adult court. Even Nathaniel Blackwood, the high-priced criminal defense lawyer hired by his dad, told Cole he might be tried as an adult. If convicted, he'd be sent to prison.

Cole couldn't believe his parents were letting this happen to him. What jerks! He hated his parents. His mom acted like a scared Barbie doll, always looking good but never fighting back or standing up to anyone. His dad was a bullheaded drinker with a temper. He figured everything was Cole's fault. Why wasn't his room clean? Why hadn't he emptied the garbage? Why hadn't he mowed the lawn? Why was he even alive?

"I never want to see your ugly faces again," Cole shouted at the lawyer and his parents after finding out he wouldn't be released. But still his parents tried to see him. Because of their divorce, they visited separately. That's how much they thought about themselves and about him, Cole thought. They couldn't even swallow their dumb pride and visit together.

During each visit, Cole relaxed on his bed and pretended to read a newspaper, completely ignoring them. He liked watching his parents, especially his dad, squirm and get frustrated. Some days his dad got so mad, he turned beet red and twitched because he couldn't lay a finger on Cole with the guards watching.

Finally his parents quit trying to visit. Even Nathaniel Blackwood quit stopping by except when hearings and depositions required his presence. Cole didn't like the lawyer. Blackwood was a stiff man and spoke artificially, as if he were addressing an audience through a microphone. Cole swore he wore starch on everything. Judging by how he walked, that included his underwear.

The only person who insisted on visiting regularly was Garvey, the stocky youth probation officer, who stopped by the detention center almost daily.

Cole couldn't figure Garvey out. He knew the probation officer was super busy, so why did he visit so often? What was his angle? Everybody had an angle—something they wanted. Until Cole could figure out what Garvey wanted, he resented the visits—he didn't need a friend or a baby-sitter.

During one visit, Garvey asked casually, "I know you're in control, Champ, but would you ever consider applying for Circle Justice?"

"What's Circle Justice?"

"It's a healing form of justice practiced by native cultures for thousands of years."

"I'm no Indian!" Cole said.

Garvey spoke patiently. "You don't have to be Native American or First Nation. Anybody can love, forgive, and heal. Nobody has a corner on that market."

"What's in it for me?"

Garvey shook his head. "If you kill my cat, normally the police fine you and that's it. We still hate each other, I still feel bad about my cat, and you're angry because you have to pay a fine. In Circle Justice, you sign a healing contract. You might agree to help me pick out a new kitten and care for it as part of the sentencing."

"Why would I want to take care of a dumb cat?"

"Because you've caused my cat and me harm. By doing something for me and for another cat, you help make things right again."

"What if I don't care about you and your dumb cat?"

"Then do it for yourself. You're also a victim. Something terrible has happened to you to make you want to kill a poor small animal."

Cole shrugged. "Feeding a dumb cat beats paying a fine."

Garvey smiled and clapped Cole on the back. "You just don't get it, do you, Champ?"

Cole ducked away from Garvey. He hated being called Champ. And he hated being touched. Nobody ever touched him except to hit him. That's how it had been as long as he could remember.

"Circle Justice tries to heal, not punish," Garvey explained. "Your lawyer might take you to a zoo to help you appreciate animals more. The prosecutor might have you watch a veterinarian operate for a day to realize the value of life. The judge might help you on the weekend to make birdhouses as repayment to the animal kingdom for something you destroyed. Even neighbors might help in some way."

"They actually do this stuff here in Minneapolis?"

Garvey nodded. "It's a new trial program. Other towns and cities are trying it, too."

"Why go to so much trouble?"

"To heal. Justice should heal, not punish. If you kill my cat, you need to become more sensitive to animals. You and I need to be friends, and I need to forgive you to get over my anger. That's Circle Justice. Everybody is a part of the healing, including people from the community—anybody who cares. But healing is much harder than standard punishment. Healing requires taking responsibility for your actions."

Cole bit at his lip. "So would this get me out of going to jail?"

"It isn't about avoiding jail," Garvey said. "You go to jail angry, you stay angry. Go with love, that's how you come back. This is all about *how* you do something, not *what* you do. Even jail can be positive if you go in with a good heart. I will say this, however. Usually the jail sentence, if there is one, is reduced under Circle Justice."

That's all Cole needed to hear. He knew what game to play. "How do I get into this Circle Justice stuff?" he asked innocently.

Garvey placed a hand on Cole's shoulder. "I'll get you an application," he said, "but you're the one who starts the process in your heart." He tapped Cole's chest. "If you don't want change, this will never work."

Cole forced himself not to pull away from Garvey's hand. "I really do want change," he said, using the innocent childish voice that had served him well countless times before.

Garvey nodded. "Okay, let's see if you're serious. I'll help you with the application."

After Garvey left the detention center that day, Cole jabbed his fist into the air. "Yes!" he exclaimed. The world was made up of suckers and fools, and today Garvey was at the top of the heap.

CHAPTER 2

THE HEAVY LOAD of supplies caused the skiff to wallow through the waves. Cole examined the boxes filled with canned foods, clothes, bedroll, ax, cooking gear, heavy rain gear, rubber boots, and even schoolwork he was supposed to complete. He chuckled. Fat chance he'd ever do any schoolwork.

Several weeks earlier, Edwin, the Tlingit elder from Drake, had built a sparse one-room wood shelter for Cole on the island. He described the interior as bare except for a small woodstove and a bed—a good place for a soul to think and heal.

Cole resented the cabin and all this gear. When his father had agreed to pay all the expenses of banishment, it was just another one of his buyouts. Cole had news for him. This was just a sorry game. He twisted harder at the handcuffs and winced at the pain. He wasn't afraid of pain. He wasn't afraid of anyone or anything. He was only playing along until he could escape. He glanced back at Garvey. This whole Circle Justice thing had been such a joke. Back in Minneapolis, he had been forced to plead guilty and ask the Circle for help changing his life.

Asking for help was a simple con job, but he hadn't liked the idea of pleading guilty. "That's like hanging myself," he had complained to Garvey.

"You can withdraw your guilty plea and go through standard justice any time you want," Garvey said. "But once you go to trial, it's too late for Circle Justice." When Cole hesitated, Garvey added, "I thought you liked being in control, Champ."

Cole didn't trust anyone, but what choice did he have? "Okay," he answered reluctantly. "But if you're lying, you'll be sorry."

Garvey feigned surprise. "Let me get this straight, Champ. You figure if I'm scared of you, you can trust me?" He smiled thinly. "You sure have a lot to learn about trust."

"Quit calling me Champ," Cole mumbled. "That's not my name." Then grudgingly he held his tongue. Nobody was going to make him lose his cool. This was a game he planned to win. "So," he asked, "how soon do I start this Circle Justice stuff?"

"You can apply, but that doesn't mean you're

automatically accepted. First the Circle committee will visit with you. They'll talk to Peter Driscal and his family, your parents, and others to decide if you're serious about wanting change. It might take weeks." Garvey hesitated. "Remember something else. You're wasting everybody's time if you don't truly want change."

Cole nodded obediently, like a little puppy that would follow every rule and jump through any hoop. When he reached the island, that would all come to a screeching stop. Then he would prove to the whole world he was nobody's fool.

Cole heard the motor slow and realized that Edwin was guiding the skiff toward a protected bay on the large island ahead. The distant green-black forests were shrouded in gray mist. Cole spotted the tiny shelter that had been built for him near the trees, above the shoreline. Black tar paper covered the small wooden structure. Cole spit again at the waves. If these fossils really thought he was going to live in that shack for a whole year, they were nuts.

As the skiff scraped the rocks, Garvey jumped out and pulled the boat ashore. Still handcuffed, Cole crawled awkwardly over the bow onto the slippery rocks. Edwin began immediately to unload the supplies.

"Why don't you take my handcuffs off and let me help?" Cole asked.

Garvey and Edwin ignored his question. One at a time they carried the heavy cardboard boxes up to the shelter and stacked them inside the door. When they finished, Edwin motioned for Cole to follow him up to the mossy bench of ground above the tide line. Cole moseyed along slowly, not catching up to Edwin until they reached the trees.

Edwin turned to Cole. "Nobody's going to baby-sit you here. If you eat you'll live. If not, you'll die. This land can provide for you or kill you." He pointed into the forest. "Winters are long. Cut plenty of wood or you'll freeze. Keep things dry, because wet kills."

"I'm not afraid of dying," Cole boasted.

Edwin smiled slightly. "If death stares you straight in the face, believe me, son, you'll get scared." He pointed to a tall plant with snakelike branches. "This island is covered with Devil's Club. Don't grab it or hundreds of tiny thistles will infect your hands and make them swell up like sausages." Edwin motioned toward the head of the bay, a quarter mile away. "That stream over there is where you get fresh water."

"Why didn't you put my camp closer to the stream?"

"Other animals come here for water, too," Edwin said. "How would you feel if a bear made its den beside the stream?"

Cole shrugged. "I'd kill it."

The potbellied elder nodded with a knowing smile. "Animals feel the same way. Don't forget that." He turned to Cole and placed a hand on his shoulder. Cole tried to pull away, but Edwin gripped him like a clamp. "You aren't the only creature here. You're part of a much bigger circle. Learn your place or you'll have a rough time."

"What is there to learn?"

"Patience, gentleness, strength, honesty," Edwin said. He looked up into the trees. "Animals can teach us more about ourselves than any teacher." He stared away toward the south. "Off the coast of British Columbia, there is a special black bear called the Spirit Bear. It's pure white and has pride, dignity, and honor. More than most people."

"If I saw a Spirit Bear, I'd kill it," Cole said.

Edwin tightened his grip as if in warning. "Whatever you do to the animals, you do to yourself. Remember that."

"You're crazy, old man," Cole said, twisting free of Edwin's grip. Edwin continued speaking calmly as if nothing had happened. "Don't eat anything unless you know what it is. Plants, berries, and mushrooms can kill you. There's a book in with the supplies to study if you want to learn what is safe to eat. I suggest you read every word. Life is up to you now. I don't know how it was for you in the big city, but up here you live and die by your actions. We'll be out to check on you in a couple of days. After that, Garvey will head home and I'll drop off supplies every few weeks. Any questions?"

Cole smirked. He didn't plan on eating any shrubs or berries. "Why did you bring me out so far?" he asked mockingly. "Were you afraid I'd escape?"

Edwin looked out across the bay and drew in a deep breath. "Years ago, I was brought here myself when my spirit got lost. This is a good place to find yourself."

"This place sucks!" Cole mumbled.

Edwin pulled out a key and turned Cole roughly around to remove his handcuffs. "Anger keeps you lost," he said, as he started back toward the shelter. "You can find yourself here, but only if you search."

Rubbing at the raw skin on his wrists, Cole followed.

Garvey stood outside the shelter as they walked up to it. He held out a small bundle to Cole.

"What's this?" Cole asked, unfolding a heavy wool blanket, woven with colorful blue-and-red images of a totem pole.

"Tlingits call it at.óow."

"At.óow?" Cole repeated.

"Like 'a towel' without the L," Garvey said. "At.óow is something you inherit. This blanket has been handed down for many generations in my family. It once belonged to one of our chiefs and is a link to our ancestors. You can't own at.óow. You are only its caretaker for a time. If you accept this at.óow from me, you must promise to care for it and someday pass it on to someone else you trust."

"You saying you trust me?"

Garvey nodded. "If you promise to care for it, I'll believe you. A man is only as good as his word." Garvey looked Cole in the eyes. "Do you promise me you'll care for this at.óow?"

Cole tucked the blanket under his arm. "Yeah, sure, whatever you want."

Sadly, Garvey placed a hand on Cole's shoulder. "Don't waste this chance, Cole."

Cole felt a sudden rush of anger and jerked away. Why did everybody always have to touch him? He didn't need anyone's help. What he needed was for the world to butt out. "Aren't you guys ever leaving?" he snapped.

Edwin and Garvey turned and walked to the skiff. Edwin crawled aboard first. When he was seated, Garvey shoved the small boat off the slick gray rocks and jumped aboard himself. Edwin yanked the starter rope, and the outboard roared to life.

As the skiff motored from the bay, the fading whine of the engine floated out across the choppy waters. In the distance, Garvey waved good-bye. Cole waved back, grinning. This far away, they couldn't see the extended middle finger he brandished at them.

Cole watched as the boat faded to a mere speck outside the bay, then he reached down and picked up a rock. He threw it toward the horizon with a hard grunt. Finally he was alone. For almost three months, he had been kept in detention, guarded twenty-four hours a day. For almost three months, he had put up with the adults from the Circle Justice committee. What fools. They had kept stopping by, asking questions that were a joke. Any moron could figure out what they wanted to hear.

"Why should we believe you're sincere?" several committee members had asked during their visits.

Cole wanted to say, "'Cause if you don't, I'll knock your fat heads off." Instead, he meekly said, "You shouldn't," keeping his face as serious as he could. "I've really screwed things up. Hurting someone really made me think a lot." He'd pause for effect, then add, "I wish I could trade places with Peter. I really do. That's what I deserve."

Cole had grown impatient watching the visitors jot notes in their silly little folders. What a waste of time. They were probably afraid to try him as an adult and send him to jail.

"Why can't they make up their minds?" he complained to Garvey during one of his visits. "What are they waiting for?"

"Things take time," Garvey answered. "The Circle needs to know if you're committed to wanting change. Some think you still have an attitude." Garvey grinned. "I can't imagine where they got that idea, Champ. Can you?"

"I told them I wanted to change," Cole said, his voice edgy. "What more do they want?"

"Talk is cheap. They want you to walk your talk."

"How can I prove anything sitting in this stinking place?"

"Think about it, Einstein. What if it turns out you're nothing more than a baby-faced con? What then?" Garvey threw up his hands. "A lot of people have already paid dearly for your anger and lies. You have bigger problems than getting out of this place."

"Yeah, like what?"

"If you're accepted for Circle Justice, who's going to be your sponsor? The committee requires some person to go through the process with you."

"I thought you would help me," Cole said, letting his irritation show.

Garvey shook his head. "I don't invest time in losers. Unless you're one hundred and ten percent committed to this change, you're wasting my time and everybody else's—you're better off in jail." Garvey gave Cole a playful shove. "Make up your mind, Champ. The world's getting tired of wait-ing."

Cole wanted to punch Garvey's teeth into the next county, but instead he forced a smile. After Garvey left, Cole's fists tightened until his knuckles turned white.

It was late afternoon when the boat's outline dis-appeared and the faint moaning of the outboard melted into the quiet. Sudden hot tears clouded Cole's vision. This was called Circle Justice, but it was no different than being in a jail. Once again he was being abandoned by people who wanted to get rid of him. His parents were probably glad he was a million miles from their world. They wanted him locked up like a caged animal.

Cole felt a familiar rage building inside him. The last time he had felt like this was back in his small detention cell. One afternoon, after he had refused to do the schoolwork they brought to him, his television privileges had been revoked. Cole purposely isolated himself in his room, sitting sullenly. His anger smoldered like a lit fuse.

He fantasized about how he would get even with everybody if he ever got free. His rage ignited. Cole jumped to his feet and stormed across the cell. He tipped over his metal-framed bed and started hitting the wall harder and harder. Soon blood from his scraped knuckles smeared the concrete.

Finally Cole fell to the floor beside the toilet, sobbing. He stared at his bleeding knuckles. Somebody would pay for this.

He was still huddled on the cell floor hours later when Garvey had stopped by. Garvey walked thoughtfully around the overturned bed, then headed back toward the door.

Cole looked up. "Leaving already?"

"I'm tired of being around someone who blames the world for all his problems."

"So you think it's my fault?"

"I think the world isn't always a fair place.

The sooner you get that through your thick skull, the sooner you can get on with your life."

"So does this mean you're not going to be my sponsor?" Cole blurted.

Garvey shrugged. "It means you need to make up your mind if you want change."

"I already told you I did," Cole said.

Garvey glanced down at Cole's bruised and swollen knuckles. "Are the walls getting the best of your fights?"

"I fell," Cole said, wishing he could wipe the corny smile off Garvey's face and show him what fists were really for. "I hurt them falling." He took a deep breath. He wasn't going to let Garvey sucker him into getting mad and blowing this chance to avoid jail. "Are you going to be my sponsor or not?" he demanded. "I'm not going to beg."

Garvey stopped in the doorway and turned. He looked Cole straight in the eyes. "I'll help you, but don't waste my time. You understand? I don't have time for losers."

Cole mustered a serious face. "I won't."

"Okay," Garvey said. As he left, he called back, "Hey Champ, try falling on your fists sometime."

Standing all alone on the shore, Cole felt his anger smoldering. Soon it would explode like gunpowder. As the fuse burned shorter, he tore off his clothes, turned each piece right side out, and dressed again. Now the game was over and he was in charge. He turned his back on the shimmering water and headed across the rocks.

Driftwood, seaweed, and shells lay scattered among the basketball-sized rocks. Cole picked up a chunk of driftwood and flung it hard. The shelter filled with supplies was a buyout, something that allowed his parents and everyone else to pretend they had helped him. They hadn't done squat, Cole thought. He would rather die than spend a single night in their dumb hut, playing their stupid game.

He swore as he neared the shelter. Spewing a barrage of venomous curses, he took the blanket Garvey had given him and flung it to the ground. No more games. He barged through the door of the shelter and glared around with wildness in his eyes. Beside the stack of cardboard boxes sat a gallon of white gas for use in his lantern. Cole unscrewed the top. Recklessly, he splashed the gas over the supplies. He dumped the remaining fuel on the shelter walls.

Ripping open boxes, he found matches, then, swaying on his feet, he pulled out a single match. He walked outside and stared at the supplies and at the shelter. His vision blurred. Rage controlled his tight grip on the match. It controlled the defiant flare of his nostrils and the striking of the match against the box. Rage controlled Cole's hand as he drew back, paused for a split second, and then flipped the lighted match inside the shelter.

The gas ignited, and flames spread quickly into a steady blaze that crept over the boxes. Yellow flames turned orange and red, then burned with streaks of blue. As the fire became an inferno, Cole tried to swallow the bitter taste that had come to his mouth.

CHAPTER 3

C OLE STARED SULLENLY into the fire, then let his gaze wander. He had wanted revenge but felt little joy from this act. Overhead eagles drifted on the air currents. In the bay, a mother seal played with her spotted pups as a golden sun peeked through the gray overcast and glinted off the waves. "This place sucks!" Cole mumbled as the breeze drifted sparks upward like wandering stars. He stared back into the crackling, red-hot flames, and his anger burned.

Cole rocked back and forth on his feet. Nobody cared about him. Nobody understood him. Nobody knew what it was like living with parents who wished he wasn't alive. It angered Cole when people pretended they did. His parole officer was one of those people. Once Garvey had shown up at the detention center on his day off, wearing cutoffs and a T-shirt. He carried a brown paper grocery bag. Without saying hello, he set the bag on the small concrete table in Cole's cell and sat himself down on the edge of the bed. "So," he said, "tell me exactly what it is you don't like about your life."

"Any moron can figure that out," Cole grumped, turning his back on Garvey. In the summer's stifling heat, the room seemed airless and threatening.

"Okay, explain it to this moron," Garvey said. "I'm pretty dense, you know. Your police file makes for pretty dull reading."

Not wanting to sit anywhere near Garvey, Cole slouched to the floor against the wall. "You don't get it, do you? My parents are divorced and don't give a rat if I live or die. All they care about is themselves. Nobody cares about me. All my life I've been dumped on."

"A lot of people can say that," Garvey said. "Be more specific."

"'Be more specific,'" Cole mimicked. "Last year I went out for wrestling. I had to beg my parents to come watch me. It was like they were ashamed of me."

"Did they ever come to see you?"

"Yeah, after I got mad enough. And then I lost. You'd have thought I lost on purpose the way Dad acted." When Garvey didn't answer, Cole said, "So, have you heard enough?"

"I'm still listening."

Cole didn't know why he was spilling his guts to Garvey, but he fought back tears as he continued. "All my parents do is drink. They hate me. Do you know what it's like waking up every morning knowing you're not good enough? There are only two things wrong with me—everything I do and everything I say. They'll never be happy until I'm dead."

After an awkward silence, Garvey eyed Cole. He spoke quietly. "There's still one thing more, isn't there?"

Cole hesitated. "It's none of your business!"

"I know how you're feeling," Garvey said.

Cole leaped to his feet and glared at Garvey. "You *don't* know how I'm feeling!" he shouted. "You don't know what it's like being hit over and over until you're so numb you don't feel anything!"

Garvey nodded slowly. "I *do* know what that's like. Is it your dad who hits you?"

Cole turned to face the wall. "He drinks until he turns into a monster. Mom just gets drunk and pretends nothing has happened. It's like a bad dream I can't wake up from."

Garvey stood up and reached into the brown paper bag he had brought with him. One by one he pulled out groceries and set them on the small cement table.

"What are you doing?" Cole asked.

Garvey ignored the question as he laid out salt, flour, eggs, baking soda, a bottle of water, sugar, butter, and molasses. Cole wiped sweat from his forehead. The stuffy room felt like a furnace.

"Okay," said Garvey, finishing. "Taste everything on the table."

"No way," Cole grumped. "I'm not eating that crap."

"You surprise me," Garvey said. "You're actually afraid of a little bad taste."

"I'm not afraid of anything," Cole boasted, standing and approaching the table. One by one he sampled each item, tasting first the flour, sugar, and baking soda. He purposely took big mouthfuls to prove nothing bothered him. Casually he drank some thick molasses. He stared straight at Garvey as he bit off a chunk of butter and swallowed it. When he came to the eggs, he picked one up, tilted his head back, and broke it raw into his mouth. He downed it with a single swallow. He finished by shaking salt directly into his mouth.

"So," Garvey asked. "How did everything taste?"

"Gross." Cole took a long swig of water from the bottle. "What did you expect?"

Garvey reached back into the bag. "I want you to taste one more thing." He unwrapped a small baked cake with creamy frosting and broke off a large piece. "Here," he said. "Eat this if you dare."

Cole wolfed down the moist piece of cake, eyeing Garvey the whole time. "So what does all this prove?"

Garvey shrugged. "Did you like the cake?"

"It was okay."

"I baked it this morning, using the same ingredients you tasted on the table."

"Yeah, so?" Cole said.

"What ingredients should I have left out?"

"None," Cole said. "That's a dumb question."

"But you said the ingredients tasted gross."

Cole let his irritation show. "Not mixed together, stupid."

Garvey stood and walked wearily to the door. His shoulders sagged forward as if tired from a long hike. Leaving the cake and all the ingredients on the table, he let himself out the steel door without saying good-bye.

Cole walked sullenly around the room. Cursing, he swept his arm across the table and sent the baking ingredients flying. Eggs smashed. Wrappings broke open. Plastic containers ricocheted off the wall. In seconds the small room looked bombed. Cole kicked at the butter, flour, sugar, and baking soda. Sticky molasses and egg whites coated his shoes as he picked up the cake and flung it hard at the steel door. "The cake sucks!" he shouted. "And so does my life!"

Inch by inch the billowing flames devoured the supplies and the shelter. Cole chuckled, then laughed out loud. As the searing flames surged and rolled higher along the sides of the shelter, his laughter grew hysterical. By the time the flames engulfed the wooden hut and licked up into open air, Cole had lost all control.

His wild laughter mocked the world and everyone he had ever known. It mocked the loneliness. It mocked every bully that had ever picked on him. He laughed at every time he had ever been teased, every time he'd been arrested, every time his parents had argued. He laughed at all the times he'd been beaten by his drunken father, or been ignored by his drunken mother. These were the ingredients in his cake, and they sucked! Cole didn't care anymore. His life was beyond caring.

With Cole's laughter, hot tears escaped his reddened and angry eyes and flooded his cheeks. This banishment was the ultimate hurt—worse than his father's fists and belt, worse than his mother's never caring. This was the hurt of being alone and unwanted.

The flames of the burning shelter rumbled like a freight train and sucked at the air. Thick smoke poured from the doorway and boiled upward from the blaze. Still Cole kept laughing like a madman. Not until the flames began to subside did his manic laughter fade. Only then did he let his attention stray from the fire. The first thing he saw was the at.óow, the brightly colored blanket given to him by Garvey. It rested unharmed in the grass nearby.

Shielding his face from the burning heat, Cole snatched up the at.óow, and with one swift motion, flung it toward the fire. In the same motion, he turned away from the flames and ran toward the shoreline. No one in the Healing Circle had known how strongly he could swim. Not even Garvey.

The only person who knew was his father. He was the one who had forced Cole to go out for the swim team because that is what he himself had done in high school. But no matter how well Cole swam, his father criticized him. "You swim like you have lead up your butt," he'd scream as Cole swam—if he managed to show up at all.

Cole studied the bay as he removed his shoes

and pulled off his clothes. He stood in his under-wear and stared out across the waters. The boat had brought him west from Drake. Now, with the afternoon sun setting behind him, he fixed his eyes on the first island to the east. He could swim island to island, stopping at each to warm up, eat, and sleep. Sooner or later there would be a pass-ing boat to take him back to the mainland. Nobody would ever find him, and no one would ever again tell him what to do.

Cole waded into the light surf. His breath caught when the waves reached his chest. The icy transparent water was colder than he had expected, but he plunged forward and began stroking. He knew he could not survive forever in the frigid water. Every minute counted now, and he needed to swim hard.

Rhythmically, he reached out, each stroke taking him farther away from his island prison. As Cole swam, he thought about Garvey and the stupid cake demonstration. And he thought about his application for Circle Justice. It had been a full three weeks after he'd submitted the application before Garvey had casually said, "Well, Champ, you've been accepted for Circle Justice. Now what are you going to do with this chance?"

"It's about time."

"I hope the committee knows what they're

getting into," Garvey said.

"This was your idea," Cole shot back.

Garvey nodded. "So, are you going to disappoint them?"

"Don't worry about me," Cole said. "How soon can I get out of this stink hole?"

"First the Keepers will prepare for the Hearing Circle, where everybody gets together to look for solutions."

"Who exactly will be there?"

"Anybody who wants to help."

"Who would want to help me?"

"Might be your parents, the lawyers, the judge, myself, community members, maybe even your classmates at school. Anybody can be a part of the Circle if they want to help find a solution."

"My parents—that's a joke," Cole scoffed. "They don't care if I'm dead or alive." When Garvey didn't answer, Cole asked, "Will Peter be there?"

Garvey shrugged. "It's up to him. He may not be ready to forgive you."

"I don't care if he forgives me."

Garvey rubbed the back of his neck, then glanced up toward the ceiling. "How come everything is always about you? This forgiveness isn't for you. Until Peter forgives you, he won't heal."

"Maybe if he forgives me, everyone will forget about what I did and I can get out of this pit faster."

Garvey stood to leave. "Forgiving isn't forgetting, *Chump!*"

CHAPTER 4

B Y THE TIME Cole paused to catch his breath, he found himself outside the bay, angling toward the next island, maybe a mile away. The icy water numbed him deeper with each breath. He gulped at the air. He had to make it before he froze to death. His arms ached, but he continued stroking, even as his mind wandered.

Following Cole's acceptance for Circle Justice, preparation meetings, called Circles of Understanding, took place. Each meeting was considered a Healing Circle but had a different name, depending on what was being discussed and who attended. There were Talking Circles, Peacemaking Circles, and Community Circles. Eventually there would be Bail Circles and Sentencing Circles.

"Is everything always in a circle?" Cole had asked Garvey.

"Why not?" Garvey said. "Life is a circle."

"Do I have to go to all these meetings?"

Garvey shook his head. "The organizers of the Circles are called Keepers. When the Keepers meet with people like Peter and his family, you're not allowed."

"Why do they meet with them?"

"If the Driscals realize that the Circle allows them to have a voice in decisions, and that forgiveness can help Peter to heal, they may also join the Circle."

"You mean they might help decide my sentence?"

Garvey nodded. "Maybe."

"They'll hang me," Cole said. "I'm dead."

"I think you've already hung yourself," Garvey answered.

Once preparations were ready for the first Hearing Circle, notices were sent out and meetings were held in the basement of the public library. Cole scratched nervously at his stomach as he entered the library the first night. He didn't know what to expect as the guard removed his handcuffs outside the meeting room and let him walk in alone. The guard remained in the hallway.

The woman who called herself the Keeper met Cole and shook his hand. "Thanks for coming tonight," she said pleasantly. She wore blue jeans and a flannel shirt, even though she was old enough to be Cole's grandmother.

"I didn't have much choice," Cole mumbled, as he seated himself. He picked at the edge of his chair as he watched complete strangers file in and choose seats. The number of chairs made it obvious the Hearing Circle involved a lot more people than the other meetings. To make matters worse, Cole knew that tonight he might see Peter for the first time since the beating.

Each new arrival greeted him and all the others warmly. Everybody acted as if they were friends. Cole played their game and nodded politely, but he noticed that nobody sat beside him. Several kept eyeing him curiously.

He recognized one man as Judge Tanner. The last time Cole had seen him, the judge had been wearing a black robe at the arraignment hearing in juvenile court when Cole first pleaded guilty. Tonight Judge Tanner wore no robe and was dressed in blue jeans and a sweater.

Cole's father and their lawyer, Nathaniel Blackwood, entered together, wearing dark three-piece suits and ties. They looked completely out of place. The lawyer looked as if he'd been dipped in plastic. The two nodded to Cole and seated themselves on his immediate left. Cole ignored them.

Cole's mother arrived alone and seated herself on his right. She wore a party dress. Not a single hair on her head was out of place. That's all this was, Cole thought bitterly. This was just another social event. She had probably spent a couple of hours getting ready. Nothing, however, could cover up the frightened look in her eyes. Cole guessed she had probably downed a few drinks before coming, something to calm her nerves. Cole squirmed in his seat. His parents hadn't even acknowledged each other.

When Garvey arrived, he sat nearby. Shifting nervously in his chair, Cole nodded to Garvey as he watched more strangers enter and be seated. It seemed like the whole world was showing up. And why not? The Keepers had posted a notice on the library bulletin board with an open invitation to anybody who wanted to participate.

Cole tapped his shoe against the leg of the chair. Why hadn't they just gone out in the street and hollered, "Hey, everybody, come help make fun of Cole Matthews!" At least none of his classmates had shown up, Cole thought. They probably knew what he'd do to them if they did. Then Cole heard more people come in, and turned, to see Peter walk in with his parents and their lawyer.

Peter walked awkwardly, shuffling his feet and

glancing timidly around the room. His lawyer looked the same age as Cole's mom but walked with her head up and shoulders squared. Almost immediately, she picked Cole out of the Circle and eyed him. He glanced down.

Nearly two dozen people had joined the Circle by the time the Keeper stood to begin. She smiled pleasantly. "Everybody please stand and hold hands," she said.

Cole didn't like holding hands with his parents, one on each side. His hands were clammy, and he found himself comparing his mother's frightened, weak squeeze to his father's iron-hard grip.

As the Keeper bowed her head, Cole peeked and caught Peter peeking back. He narrowed his eyes threateningly, and Peter looked away. Cole grinned until he realized Peter's lawyer was watching him.

"Great Maker and Healer, hear this prayer," began the Keeper in a soft voice. "Tonight we gather because our community has been hurt. Grant wisdom and patience as we search for wellness. Amen."

As the Circle sat down, the Keeper drew in a deep slow breath, looking around to acknowledge each person. Still smiling, she said, "Well, I see many new faces here tonight." She glanced directly at the two lawyers and Judge Tanner. "Let me remind *everybody*, we are not here to win or lose. Justice often fails because it seeks to punish, not to heal. Jails and fines harden people."

Cole found himself nodding.

The Keeper paused. "We call this Circle Justice, but we really seek wellness. We try to meet the needs of both the offender and the victim." The Keeper looked directly at Cole and his family, then at Peter and his family. "Circle Justice is for those ready for healing. It's not an easy way out. In fact, a healing path is often much harder."

The Keeper held up a feather. "This feather symbolizes respect and responsibility. No one must speak without this feather. When you hold this feather in your hand, speak honestly from your heart." She chuckled. "I hope I'm not being long-winded, because talking too long tells others that you don't respect their right to speak. Respect others as much as yourself. When the feather comes to you, speak only if you wish to. This circle carries only two obligations—honesty and respect."

The Keeper fixed her gaze on Cole. "Cole Matthews, you have a long history of anger, growing more violent until you severely injured Peter Driscal. Even now, Peter continues therapy for injuries."

Cole squirmed in his chair. He didn't like being talked to with a bunch of people staring at him.

The Keeper raised her voice slightly and turned to the group. "Our challenge is to return wellness, not only to Peter Driscal, but also to Cole Matthews and to our community. We'll pass the feather several times tonight, introducing ourselves, expressing concerns, and offering ideas for healing and repairing the harm." The Keeper handed the feather to the first person seated on her left side.

"I'm Gladys Swanson, and I'm the mother of four children here in Minneapolis," the lady began. "I want to help make our community better because this is the community where I'm raising my own children."

"I'm Frank Schaffer," the next person said. "This is the first real opportunity I've had to help change the violence in our city."

One by one, the people around the circle held the feather and spoke.

Cole's mother fingered the feather nervously during her turn. "I'm Cindy Matthews, Cole's mom," she said. "I'm here because I don't know what to do anymore. It's gotten so hard." She paused, her bottom lip trembling, then handed the feather to Cole.

The room grew extra quiet, and Cole's face warmed. Squeaking chairs and shuffling shoes broke the anxious silence. Cole coughed to clear his throat. A lot depended on his next words. "Uh, I'm Cole Matthews, and I'm here because I really screwed up," he said. "I know what I did was wrong, and I want Peter to know I'm sorry for everything." Cole sniffled purposely, rubbing at his nose for effect. "I want to ask this Circle to help me get over my anger."

Cole handed the feather to his father as he glanced around the group. He liked the reactions he saw. People heard what they wanted to hear. Tonight the group wanted to believe he was sorry—he could see it in their eyes.

Cole's father sat up taller in his chair. "I'm William Matthews," he announced importantly. "I'm here to make sure that my son never causes problems again." He turned and glared at Cole. "This is all going to end now."

Cole ignored his father.

Next, Nathaniel Blackwood received the feather. He held it loosely in his fingers as if it were a cigarette and cleared his throat loudly. "Yes, what Cole did was wrong, but kids will be kids. Considering Cole's detention to date, we feel he should be released to parole and to the supervision of one of his parents. He needs a family, not a jail cell." The lawyer handed the feather on.

As the feather moved from person to person, Cole kept glancing at Peter. The thin red-haired boy stared at the floor. When he was handed the feather, Peter looked up fearfully and mumbled, "I'm Peter Driscal, and I'm here 'cause I got beat up." His speech was slow and halting. His eyes darted around the Circle as he passed the feather quickly to his mother.

Cole studied Peter. Peter hadn't sounded like this before. Cole wiped his sweaty hands on his pants. It wasn't like he had meant to hurt anyone. Besides, this wouldn't have happened if Peter had kept his mouth shut.

CHAPTER 5

ONCE CLEAR OF the bay, Cole swam even harder. Misty rain roughed the water as waves washed over his head. When he stopped to rest, his breath came in ragged gasps. His numb limbs felt wooden and stiff, moving awkwardly as if disconnected from his body. Cole turned to look back.

At first his mind rejected what he saw—he was still at the mouth of the bay. He shook his head to clear the illusion, but it was no illusion. This was the same spot he had been at a thousand strokes earlier. But how could it be? The wind and waves hadn't been that strong, yet even as he struggled to tread water with his numb limbs, he found himself drifting back toward the shoreline.

In that instant, Cole realized his mistake. His anger had so clouded his thinking, he hadn't considered the incoming tide. With every stroke forward, a giant invisible hand had pushed him two strokes backward into the bay, returning him toward the shore.

A sharp cramp gripped Cole's leg, then his other leg started cramping. He gasped for breath and panicked. He had to make it back to land. Any land. Frantically he flailed at the water.

Struggling did little to affect Cole's movement, but on the incoming tide he steadily drifted closer to shore. He fought only to keep his head above water. When the rocky bottom bumped against his feet, he kept thrashing his lifeless limbs. Again and again his feet struck the rocky bottom, and pain shot up his legs. Finally he quit fighting and let the waves push his body into shallow water.

A wave broke over his head, and he came up gagging and spitting salt water. He tried to lift himself, but his arms collapsed. Finally, using only his elbows, he squirmed and crawled his way over the slippery rocks and up onto the grassy ground above the tide line. There he lay spent and shivering, his body bruised, his cold skull throbbing in rhythm with his heartbeat.

Cole had lost all track of time and struggled to think. All he could conjure up were fleeting notions: He couldn't stand up. He needed warmth. It was almost dark. He felt pain. One thought repeated: He needed warmth. He knew there was no warmth, and yet he remembered flames. Where were the flames? He had to find them.

Cole tried to stand up, but his legs collapsed under him. Imagining a fire, he dragged his way forward again on his belly. His legs pulled behind him like worthless anchors. It was hard in the gathering darkness to make out shapes. The waves, the shoreline, the trees, the bay, all existed like parts of a puzzle.

Cole rested again until the throbbing in his head had disappeared. His head felt hollow, his mind empty. One detached thought kept coming back to him: There had been flames. But where? Night had come quickly, and Cole scanned the dark shadows around him, sensing a vague familiarity. Again he tried to stand but couldn't. He dragged himself forward one last time, then collapsed.

Slowly the cold disappeared. Lying belly down in the darkness, Cole felt his legs and chest sting as if they were on fire. Then he became aware of another feeling. Stronger than any burning in his arms and belly, more haunting than the darkness that surrounded him, was the realization that he was alone, totally alone with himself. And it scared him.

Sometime during the night, Cole drifted into a fitful sleep. When he awoke, darkness still hid the island. His first conscious sense was pain. His toes, hands, elbows, chest, legs, all ached. What had happened? Vaguely he remembered burning the supplies and the shelter, and then trying to escape by swimming. After that he remembered the tide and crawling up the rocky shore. There had been terrible cold, then more crawling. Then he recalled his skin burning. After that, a damning loneliness.

Cole breathed in the cold, damp night air. Where was he now? The air smelled of salt, seaweed, and something burnt. Then he slept again. When he awoke the next time, dawn had crept into the sky. Lifting one arm, he found it covered with black ash. He was lying nearly naked, squarely in the ashes of the burned shelter.

He gathered his strength and struggled to his feet. The world seemed to tilt and spin. In the dawn light, billowy clouds mounded against the far horizon like a snowdrift. The warm ash stuck to the raw scrapes on Cole's chest and legs. Blood crusted his elbows and knees, and his dry mouth kept him from swallowing. Every joint in his body ached.

As he wavered on his weakened legs, Cole became aware of a presence. Not movement, only a lurking presence. Grimacing, he searched the trees and shore. At first nothing appeared different or out of place. Then something large and white broke the smooth pattern of the shoreline. He squinted, and the image cleared.

A bear. A white bear.

Out across the water, on the point of shoreline near the opening of the bay, a massive white bear stood as motionless as a statue, facing him. Morning light glinted off its shiny white fur and made it glow. The bear stood patiently, proud, nose forward, ears alert. Cole kept blinking his eyes. Could this possibly be one of the Spirit Bears Edwin had spoken of? He had said they lived hundreds of miles to the south on a different island. And yet what else could it be?

Shivering in only his underwear, Cole crouched and picked up a rock. This Spirit Bear didn't have any right to stare at him. It didn't have pride, dignity, and honor like Edwin had said. It was just a mangy animal. Cole flung the rock, even though the bear was nearly a quarter mile away. "Keep staring, I'll kill you," he shouted.

What really angered Cole about the bear was that it stood there frozen on the shoreline without any sign of fear. It defied him. He looked around for some kind of weapon. In the ashes he spotted the charred blade of a hunting knife from one of the boxes. He picked it up and turned back toward the Spirit Bear.

It had disappeared.

Cole searched the trees, but the bear was gone. Puzzled, he tossed the knife back on the ground. "I ever see you again, you're dead," he vowed. "I'll teach you to be afraid of me."

As he turned back toward the ashes, another bright object caught his attention. Not ten feet away lay the colorful red-and-blue blanket Garvey had given him. What had he called it? At.óow? It rested near some tall grass, completely untouched by the flames. Cole picked it up and examined it with his sore fingers. Had he missed when he threw the at.óow into the flames? Shrugging, he wrapped the blanket around his shoulders. He hobbled on his bruised feet down to where he had left his shoes and clothes.

Cole felt no regret for having burned the supplies and the shelter. Nor did he regret hurting Peter. This was all somebody else's fault. If it weren't for his parents, Peter, and the stupid Healing Circle, he wouldn't even be here. Somebody would pay for what was happening. He would get revenge, especially against those who had wanted him in jail. People like Peter's lady lawyer. He hated her.

Cole remembered the first time he had seen her hold the feather in the Circle. She waved it like a wand and pointed it directly at him. "That boy is dangerous," she said. "Next time he might kill someone. This Circle Justice has its place, but I oppose any plan that does not isolate Cole Matthews."

Cole didn't like someone accusing him. He hated sitting in a room across from the slimeball creep he had used as a punching bag. And he hated being around his parents and the high-priced lawyer they had hired for him. The room felt stuffy, and he dug at the woven fabric on his chair with his fingernail. Circle Justice stunk! Each word spoken in the Circle was like kindling added to his smoldering anger.

"Cole must go to jail and get anger counseling," somebody said. "He's proved he can't be trusted."

"Cole is a risk to our children and to our community," another person in the Circle said. "We can't risk his release."

It was the next voice that made Cole explode. His father held the feather, toying with it in his fingers. "We've always wanted the best for Cole," he said. "His mother and I have devoted our lives to him, but he—"

"That's bull!" Cole shouted suddenly, although he wasn't holding the feather. "You drink until you can't stand up, and you're gone all the time. A devoted parent doesn't whip his kid until a shirt can't hide all the bruises!"

CHAPTER 6

C OLE'S CLOTHES FELT damp and stiff when he
picked them up from where he'd left them
on the shoreline. As he struggled to pull
them on, he chuckled. He couldn't quit thinking
about the Circle Justice meetings. He still remembered how surprised the group had been when
he called his dad a liar. Every eye in the group had
focused on his father, who turned red and stammered angrily, "We *have* devoted our lives to
Cole. We—"

"All you care about is *you*!" Cole interrupted.
"Look how you're dressed. Nobody else here is—"

"That's not true," protested his father. He
grabbed Cole's arm roughly, but then let go. He
glared at Cole and pointed the feather in his face.
"You control your mouth, son, or I'll—"

"Or you'll what?" Cole taunted. "Beat me?"

Cole's father jumped to his feet. "I don't beat
you, and you know that." His face flushed red. "I've
given you swats when you've deserved them."

The Keeper stepped forward into the center of the Circle and held up her hand, but Cole ignored her. "You're still lying!" he shouted. "You're usually too drunk to know your own name!" Cole knew these words guaranteed him a terrible beating the next time he was alone, but still he taunted his father with a smirk. He didn't plan on there being any next time. The first chance he had, he would run away.

Again the Keeper held up her hand for order, but Cole's father raised his voice even louder. "I've given you every—"

Nathaniel Blackwood reached up and pulled Cole's father forcefully back to his seat. The Keeper stepped forward and held her hand out for the feather. "Please," she said firmly. The gentle calm had left her voice and face. Her chin was rigid.

Embarrassed, Cole's father surrendered the feather.

The Keeper turned and spoke to the whole Circle. "We *must* respect the feather. This symbolizes respect for others and respect for ourselves." As if handling a priceless gem, the Keeper handed the feather carefully to Cole. "Now you may speak."

Cole tried to be calm, but his voice shook and his face felt hot. "We aren't supposed to lie when we hold the feather, but my dad just lied. My parents don't have the time of day for me. I'm just in their way, especially since they split up. I bet my dad can't even tell you when my birthday is." Cole grabbed a deep breath to control himself. He turned to his mother and placed the feather in her lap. "Mom, tell them how Dad beats on me when he's drunk."

Cole's mother dusted imaginary specks off her dress, then picked up the feather hesitantly. She opened her mouth to speak, but a quick glance at her husband brought a frightened look to her eyes. She quickly passed the feather on to Garvey without saying anything.

Garvey held the feather and pursed his lips with a troubled stare. "I don't know how life gets so mixed up," he began. "Some juvenile delinquents become our most successful citizens, while others crowd our prisons. What's the difference?" He paused. "Cole has will and courage, but he also has ugly anger. So what do we do with him? Do any of us know what caused that anger? And what if those same events had happened to each of us? How would we have reacted?" He paused for an uncomfortably long moment.

A muted murmur rippled around the Circle.

"Seriously," Garvey said, turning first to Peter, then to Cole. "I don't know how to heal emotional and physical damage. Scars run deep." Garvey stared intently at Cole's father, who sat unflinching. "I do know this: Cole isn't the only problem here tonight. He is only a symptom of a family and a community that has somehow broken down. If we can't find solutions, we all fail, we all share the guilt, and we all pay a terrible price."

Nobody had anything more to say until the feather reached Peter's lawyer. The woman faced Cole directly. "We don't know all the reasons for Cole's anger, but we do know he's out of control. Any solution found by this Circle must protect society and make Cole totally responsible for his actions." She handed the feather to Peter's mother.

Peter's mother also turned to look straight at Cole. "Because of you, I have a son now who . . ." Her voice broke. "I have a son who has speech and coordination problems. He wakes up at night screaming with nightmares. Five years, ten years, even a hundred years of jail can't change that. But never again should any other parent have to worry about this happening to their child. Not sending you to jail would be a huge mistake."

Cole sat tight-lipped. The jail talk was getting old. If he was going to end up in jail anyway, he might as well have gone through normal justice and avoided all this Circle baloney. Suddenly he wanted out of this place. If only there weren't a guard waiting in the hallway.

Cole slouched low in his chair as the feather passed on to Peter. Peter gripped the feather with a tight fist and looked down at his lap. When a full minute had passed, the Keeper walked around and placed her hand gently on his shoulder. "Peter, would you like to tell us what you think would make things better again?"

Peter bit at his lip before speaking in a struggling, slurred voice. "I think someone should smash Cole's head against a sidewalk so he knows how it feels."

Uneasy glances followed Peter's comment. Even the Keeper's voice sounded tense as she took the feather gently from Peter's hand and returned to her place in the Circle. "Tonight, raw feelings have been exposed like plowed-up ground," she said. "But that's when you plant seeds. We now understand better the struggle we face, and share the desire to find a solution. Let's stand and hold hands again." Three hours after it began, the Keeper closed the Healing Circle with a prayer.

Cole stood but refused to hold his parents' hands. He folded his arms defiantly across his chest, causing a break in the Circle. On his left stood a liar who had beat him numb, and on his right stood a dressed-up puppet, afraid of her own shadow. Cole would not let them hold his hands and feel how sweaty they were. He would not let them pretend they loved him. Especially his dad.

If the Keeper noticed Cole's actions, she did not show it. When the prayer was finished, Cole's parents and their lawyer immediately began putting on their coats to leave. Cole's guard entered the room and took hold of Cole's elbow, motioning toward the door.

Cole jerked his arm free. "I can walk by myself."

With one swift movement, the guard pulled handcuffs from his belt and clipped Cole's wrists behind his back.

Others from the Circle turned to watch.

"What's that for?" Cole asked loudly.

"You had your choice," the guard said.

Before they could leave, Garvey walked up. "You're not buying into this Circle stuff, are you, Champ?"

Cole sneered at Garvey. "So now you read minds, huh?"

Garvey shook his head. "Actions speak louder than words."

"Whose side are you on, anyway?" Cole said.

Cole's father, standing nearby, overheard Cole's

remark. "Son, this isn't about choosing sides. This is about learning responsibility."

Before Cole could answer, Garvey said, "Yes, Mr. Matthews, this is about responsibility. By the way, when *is* your son's birthday?"

Cole's father gulped a quick breath, and his face grew flushed. "Uh, well . . . birthdays have never been a very big thing around our house," he stammered. "I think it's the beginning of July sometime." Quickly he turned and left.

"Did you hear him lie tonight when he was holding the feather?" Cole asked Garvey.

"He wasn't the only one," Garvey said, heading for the door.

Thinking about the Circle Justice meetings brought Cole's anger alive once more. If Garvey or Edwin or anybody else showed their ugly faces on the island now, they better watch out. Cole swatted at the persistent mosquitoes and studied the bay. His only mistake in trying to escape had been forgetting about the incoming tide. Next time, he would wait until the tide flowed outward. He would use the current to help carry him away from this armpit place.

Cole walked over to the small clear stream flowing out from the trees at the head of the bay. The canopy of trees, vines, deadfall, and undergrowth formed a wall of dark green vegetation that would have been hard to crawl through. How did the Spirit Bear move like a ghost through such tangled forest?

Cole knelt on the slippery rocks and drank until the chalky dryness left his mouth. Hunger gnawed at his stomach, but he ignored it. If he had to, he'd eat raw fish or grass. He'd eat anything if it helped get him off this island.

Returning to the ashes, Cole noticed faint smoke curling up from one mound. He dug carefully with a stick until he found hot coals, then scrounged dry twigs from under the tree branches. Steady blowing soon coaxed a weak flame to life. This time he would leave with his body warm and his belly full of food.

Heavy dark clouds crowded the far horizon, but clear sky overhead let the sun bathe the ground with warmth. Cole leaned his head back to soak in the sunshine. Garvey had said this area had tons of rain. What did he know, living in Minnesota? There had been a few light showers yesterday and during the night, but now the weather was great.

For the next few hours, Cole sat on the shore and studied the tide. Once the breeze ruffled the tree branches behind him, and Cole spun around, expecting the Spirit Bear again. He saw only a couple of big gray birds hopping among the branches. He snickered at how jumpy he was. What was he afraid of? The Spirit Bear wouldn't show itself now that it knew a human was around. It was the one that should be scared.

Cole discovered that high tide occurred midday and began flowing out of the bay within an hour. He knew that tides repeated themselves every twelve hours, which meant the next receding tide would be late tonight, then another this time tomorrow. Reluctantly, Cole admitted it would be best to leave tomorrow. He didn't want to swim at night.

He almost wished he could be here to see the faces of Garvey and Edwin when they returned and found him gone and everything burned to the ground. His dad's reaction would be even better. "What are you going to do, Dad?" Cole asked aloud, as if his dad were sitting beside him on the rocks. "Who are you going to sue? Who are you going to hit?"

Cole knew what his dad hated most about this whole situation was that his son wasn't something that could be fixed with a lawsuit or a stiff drink. The only solution was to hit Cole harder, and that hadn't helped, either.

Cole remembered once when he had disobeyed his father and come home late. After being strapped until his skin was raw with welts, he watched in horror as his dad paused and turned the belt around with his big knuckled hands. "You think life's a game! You think you're in charge! You think I'm a big joke!" his father shouted as he started hitting Cole again, this time with the metal buckle end.

Again and again Cole screamed, "Don't! Don't! I'm sorry I came home late. I'll obey! Please, Dad, don't! Life's not a game! Please stop!"

As Cole kept screaming, his dad kept hitting him. That night was the only time Cole's mom ever said anything in his defense. She came to the doorway, a drink in her hand. "Honey, you're hurting him," she said.

Cole's father spun around to face her. "You mind your own business or I'll use this thing on you."

Cole's mother retreated down the hall, but the strapping stopped.

Cole stood and stretched. Going to an island had seemed like a good idea after being locked up for three months. Now it seemed stupid. It was mainly Garvey's fault. After the fifth Circle meeting, when Cole had grown frustrated by all the references to jail, he had finally pleaded with the Circle members, "Why can't you just believe me when I say I'm sorry and won't ever hurt anybody again?"

Peter's lawyer had asked for the feather. "All your life you've lied, manipulated people, and tried to avoid consequences," she said. "There is absolutely no reason to believe that you have truly changed inside."

"Great, then get rid of me," Cole said. "Send me someplace where I'm not in your face and can't hurt anyone. But why do I have to go to jail?"

"Cole has a point," said Garvey. "Maybe there is some place other than prison."

"Anyplace he goes, there will be people he could assault," Peter's mother said. "It's not like we can ship Cole to the Arctic Circle."

Garvey's face came alive with thought, and he asked for the feather again. "I'm a native Tlingit," he said. "I was raised in Southeast Alaska. It is possible I could make arrangements to have Cole banished to a remote island on the Inland Passage. This is something First Nation people have done for hundreds of years. Cole could undergo a vision quest of sorts, an extended time alone to face himself and to face the angry spirits inside of him."

"Would anybody be with him?" asked the Keeper.

"No." Garvey shook his head. "Occasionally an elder would check on him. What makes banishment work is the extreme isolation. It allows the offender to spend a long period free of all friends, drugs, alcohol, and other influences that have gotten them into trouble. It's a time to think."

"For how long?" asked Judge Tanner, his voice edged with skepticism.

"Perhaps a year."

Peter's mother motioned for the feather. "Okay, let's say Cole is sentenced to some island for a year. What happens after that year if he hasn't changed? Would he go free to hurt somebody else's child?"

Garvey shook his head. "Banishment isn't a sentence. It's simply a time for Cole to walk his talk. We tell him to give more than lip service to the idea of change, but what chance does he have to prove anything if he's locked up? Sentencing would be delayed until the end of Cole's banishment. Then this same Circle could reevaluate him and decide whether he has walked his talk, and whether a sentence is still necessary."

"What do you think of this idea?" the Keeper asked Cole.

Cole shrugged. "I've spent lots of time outside. It's not like I couldn't take care of myself." He turned to Garvey. "But could I still end up going to jail after spending a whole year on some island?"

"That would be totally up to you," Garvey said. "You keep asking for a chance to prove you've changed. If you have, you have nothing to worry about."

Cole tried not to show it, but he was plenty worried.

Suddenly everybody seemed to motion for the feather at once. Rapidly the feather worked its way around the Circle. The air bristled with comments and questions, and by the time the Keeper finished her closing prayer that night, everyone had agreed that Garvey should explore to see whether the plan might actually work.

After the meeting, Garvey motioned Cole aside. "You do know that banishment is much harder than any jail cell, don't you?" he said.

"Then what's the point?" Cole asked.

"If you go to jail, I won't bet a nickel on your future."

"So what's so hard about living on some island for a while?"

Garvey smiled knowingly. "Go ahead and try it. Try manipulating a storm or lying to your hunger. Try cheating the cold."

CHAPTER 7

U NABLE TO FIND much dry wood on the ground, Cole broke lower branches directly off the trees and fed the fire. The fire smoked heavily and stung his eyes whenever it drifted his way, but at least it helped keep away the swarms of bloodthirsty mosquitoes.

As he gathered more wood for the night, Cole glanced over at Garvey's blanket lying on the ground. The at.óow would come in handy tonight if it got cold. Satisfied with the pile of wood he had gathered, Cole settled in beside the smoky, sputtering flames and gazed out toward the mouth of the bay.

Suddenly flashes of black and white sliced the water. Cole spotted the glistening keel-like fins of an orca whale guiding her young calf along the shoreline in search of food. Both surfaced repeatedly for breaths. Chuffs of air from their blowholes broke the still air.

Cole ignored the orcas and kept tending the

fire. He watched the thick white smoke drift upward like a twisted ribbon dissolving into the sky. His cheek muscles tightened, and a dull anger glazed his eyes. He felt wearier than he had ever felt before. With his hands in tight fists, he closed his eyes and shook his head back and forth, trying to clear the anger and pressure from his mind. He wanted to think straight. He *needed* to think straight.

When Cole opened his eyes once more, his breath caught.

The bear had reappeared.

Beside the water, not a hundred yards away, the Spirit Bear stood watching him with a fearless and passive stare.

"You maggot!" Cole yelled, leaping to his feet. "I'll kill you!"

He searched the ground and found the charred knife blade. He needed more than a knife. Turning his back on the bear, he walked up to the trees to find a thin, straight sapling to make a spear. As he searched, he carefully avoided the thistly Devil's Club.

When he found the perfect sapling, he hacked it off with the knife blade and sharpened the end. Balancing the spear in his hand, he nodded with satisfaction, then returned to the fire and rested the spear against a tree. Again the Spirit

Bear had vanished, but it didn't matter. If it showed its ugly face again now, it was dead!

Cole hung close to the fire the rest of the day and fed the damp wood into the flames, purposely using the smoke to help drive off mosquitoes. By late afternoon, his eyes stung and he scratched irritably at a dozen puffy bites. Hunger knotted his stomach, but he ignored the craving. Instead he hiked to the stream and drank his belly full. He kept the knife and the spear by his side. As darkness settled, the Spirit Bear failed to show itself again. Cole cut boughs off the spruce trees and fashioned a mattress beside the fire. He huddled under the at.óow, curling into a fetal position to keep warm. This day had been easy. Surviving on this island would have been a piece of cake had he wanted to stay, especially with supplies.

Cole rolled onto his back and gazed up at the sky. Stars glistened overhead like frozen fireworks. Curtains of northern lights out over the bay danced wildly under the Big Dipper. Cole turned his head and stared into the black nothingness of the shrouded woods. That was how he felt inside—empty. There was no beauty. For two hours his mind roiled with turbulent thoughts before he fell into a restless, tortured sleep.

Cole awoke during the night to strange

noises deep in the trees. A loud splash sounded in the bay. He sat up and restoked the fire. As he coaxed the flames higher, his thoughts again focused on escape.

This time his escape would end differently. He would leave midday, right after high tide. By the time he cleared the bay, the receding current would help wash him away from the island. Then it would be easy to make it to the next island. Still planning his escape, Cole again drifted off to sleep.

The next time he awoke, he opened his eyes to an eerie stillness. It was as if the sky were holding its breath. The little sounds that normally filled the night air had quieted. Cole sat up and peered toward the blackness of the tree cover. Was the Spirit Bear prowling in the shadows just beyond view?

"You mangy dog!" Cole shouted into the night.

The night remained still.

Cole lay back down and pulled the at.óow tightly around his neck. He adjusted a spruce bough poking him in his back. Still sleep refused to return. As dawn came, the black sky turned gray, then clouded over, and it began to drizzle.

Cole crawled stiffly to his feet, numb from lack of sleep. His breath showed in the crisp

morning air, and a tight knot twisted at his gut—
he needed food. The swim today would demand
energy. But first he needed to build up the fire
that had burned down to hot coals.

Cole gathered kindling as he swung his arms
and stomped his feet to warm up. He knelt and
blew into the embers. Gradually smoke curled
upward. He added more wood and coaxed the
smoke into flames, then headed out in search of
food.

He found it easier to walk on the spongy
grasses above tide line instead of over the slippery
rocks nearer the water. In one hand he held the
spear, in the other the charred knife blade. When
he reached the mouth of the bay, he spotted three
seagulls pecking at a half-eaten fish on the rocks.

He rushed toward the gulls, hollering and
swinging his arms until the strutting scavengers
abandoned their find. Squawking, they took to
the air. With the complaining gulls circling overhead, Cole picked up the remains of the fish. The
front half had been bitten cleanly off. Cole
glanced around for any sign of the Spirit Bear but
saw nothing. Still eyeing the trees, he held up his
find. The gulls had mangled the fish, but big pink
chunks of fresh meat still clung to the skeleton.

It wouldn't be quite like burgers on the grill,
but then this wasn't exactly Minneapolis,

Minnesota, either, Cole thought, heading back toward camp. As he walked, he picked dangling guts and dirt from the fish. This was the meal that would give him the energy he needed to escape.

When Cole reached camp, he jabbed the blunt end of his spear into the chest cavity of the fish and rotated it over the smoky flames. As the meat charred, Cole ripped off chunks and ate. He gorged himself until his stomach bulged, then he walked to the stream for another drink. Returning, he picked more meat from the skeleton. It might be a while before he ate again.

The steady drizzle turned to rain. Cole wished the sun would come out again. He tugged the at.óow tightly around his shoulders and circled the fire to keep away from the drifting smoke. As he added branches to keep the faltering flames alive, he watched the rain pelt the icy slate-gray waters of the bay.

If only he could wait a couple of days for better weather. But he couldn't. By then Edwin and Garvey would have returned to check on him. Cole crowded nearer to the fire. Already he had been on this island one full night. He would leave today, and he would leave warm and full of food.

With the heavy overcast, it was hard to judge time. Cole guessed it might be another three or four hours until high tide. Already he could see the water level rising. He rolled a big rock over beside the smoky flames to use as a chair. The incessant rain made the fire sputter and send up whiffs of smoke with a sweet burnt smell. Cole wrung water from the at.óow and pulled it back over his shoulders. At least the mosquitoes had disappeared.

When Cole looked up again to check the tide level in the bay, he blinked in disbelief. There, where the stream entered the bay, stood the Spirit Bear again. The huge white animal looked frozen on the shoreline, as motionless as the stones under its giant paws. It stared at Cole.

Cole picked up the makeshift spear in one hand, the knife blade in the other. Keeping his eyes on the big creature, he hurried along the shoreline toward it. This time the bear could not pull one of its disappearing acts. It would have to run to escape. But still it remained, rain dripping from its matted coat.

As Cole neared, he slowed. Any second now, the bear would turn and run. Just in case it didn't, Cole raised the spear over his shoulder.

Instead of fleeing, the bear shifted position to face Cole directly. Head hung low, it waited. Cole hesitated, then kept inching forward. It puzzled him that the bear would hold its ground. It must be bluffing. Surely it would turn and run. If it didn't, it would die. He intended to kill it. Didn't the stupid moron know that?

"Get out of my face," Cole muttered, stopping less than fifty feet away.

The bear breathed in deeply but did not move.

"Go on! Get!" Cole challenged.

Still the rain fell, and the bear remained.

Cole drew the spear back, then hesitated to glance over his shoulder. No one was watching. He could easily back away from this bear and not a single human being on the planet would ever know. Cole gripped the spear so hard his knuckles hurt. A lifetime of hurt, a lifetime of proving himself, a lifetime of anger controlled his muscles now. Again he inched forward.

Scarcely twenty feet from the bear, Cole paused one last time. Vapor from the Spirit Bear's breath puffed in tiny clouds from its wet black nose. Raindrops beaded on its white bushy hair and dripped off in miniature rivulets. The bear waited calmly as if part of the landscape, like a tree or a boulder, not conceding one inch of space.

Cole found courage in the Spirit Bear's stillness. It must be scared. Why else would it just stand there instead of attacking? Cole felt his smoldering anger ignite. He knew that soon life would be altered forever one way or another, but nothing in any cell of his being allowed him to back away. If the bear did not turn and run, that left only one alternative. "You're dead," Cole whispered.

Even as he spoke, he started forward, gripping the knife and aiming the spear at the Spirit Bear's broad white chest.

CHAPTER 8

W HEN COLE'S ADVANCE brought him
within ten feet of the Spirit Bear, he
made his move. He flung the spear with
all his strength, fully intending to kill.

A blur of white motion deflected the shaft
down into the grass as the bear lunged. Cole
never even had time to raise the knife before the
bear was on him, clubbing him down with a
powerful blow. Cole's body folded and collapsed
to the ground. Before he could roll away, another
crushing paw shoved his face into the dirt. His
jaw struck a rock.

Rolling over, then scrambling to his feet,
Cole ran toward the trees, but they offered no
protection. The bear was on him again, dragging
him down, its breath rotten. Cole gripped the
knife with his left hand and clawed with his right
at some long stalks of Devil's Club—anything to
pull himself away from the raking claws of the
bear. With each desperate grab, hundreds of tiny

thistles pierced his fingers.

He ignored the thistles as the bear sank its teeth into his thigh, lifting him like a rag doll. Cole's stomach churned, and he swung the knife wildly. Each time he stabbed the bear, its powerful jaws clamped harder. Cole felt his pelvis crack. His body went weak, and the knife slipped from his hand.

The bear dropped him to the ground and pawed at his chest as if raking leaves. Sharp claws ripped flesh with each swipe. Cole raised his right arm to ward off the attack, and teeth clamped onto his forearm. Then everything seemed to happen in slow motion.

He felt his body flop back and forth, the bear swinging him by the arm. Cole pounded the bear's face with his fist, but nothing stopped the savage attack. In desperation, he grabbed the bear's neck to free his arm from the crushing jaws. A handful of white hair pulled loose. Cole heard the loud crack of bones breaking in his forearm. Then the bear dropped him with a grunt.

Cole cowered on the ground, pain piercing his shoulder. All feeling in his right arm had disappeared. As the bear turned toward him again, Cole screamed, "No! No more!" but his words came out as coarse grunts. He collapsed onto his back.

As if finishing its attack, the Spirit Bear placed its huge paws on Cole's chest and gave a single hard shove. Air exploded from Cole's lungs. Ribs snapped.

Mouth wide open, Cole gasped but could not catch his breath. The Spirit Bear towered over him, its rank breath warm. Cole struggled to move his arms, his legs, anything to escape the white monster, but his body refused to move. Waves of nauseating pain flooded through him. Each time he gasped, pain gripped his chest and the thick sweet taste of blood filled his mouth.

For an eternity, the bear remained standing over Cole in the chilling rain. Finally it drew in a deep breath, raised its massive head, and stepped casually to the side. With a lazy shuffle, it turned away and wandered down the shoreline.

For long minutes, the world stood still. Gasping for air, Cole tried to roll to his side, but pain tore at his hip and chest. As air gradually seeped back into his lungs, he strained to raise his right arm, but his arm, like a broken branch in the grass, refused to move. The only movements Cole could make were with his left arm and his head.

The incessant rain tickled his cheeks and mixed with the blood from his mouth, dripping red by the time it hit the ground. Cole closed his eyes. Was he dying? Every movement, every breath tortured him. The blood seeping into his throat choked him. He coughed, and pain ripped at his chest. His stomach churned, and the world threatened to turn black. Cole resolved never to cough again. He would drown first.

He gazed upward and found himself under the branches of a tree in full view of the bay. The lumpy ground hurt. Barely ten feet away, seagulls strutted around, squawking, flapping their skinny wings, and picking at something in the grass.

Cole stared down at his chest. The bear's claws had raked him open. His shredded shirt exposed gashes with long strips of flesh missing. One of the gulls squawked as it stole a stringy piece of meat and skin from another gull. Cole realized the gulls were fighting over bits of his own torn flesh.

He tried to shout and wave at them, but all he managed was a lame flopping of his left hand. A dull angry grunt caught in his throat. The gulls shied a few feet, then returned to picking through the grass. In a rage, Cole tried to spit at them. The bloody mucus ran down his chin and dripped on his shoulder.

Cole licked his numb lips, but the pain made him stop—he had bitten his tongue when the bear slammed his face into the ground. He watched as one by one the gulls took to the air.

They circled out over the bay in search of better pickings.

Cole glared at them. The gluttonous seagulls had brazenly eaten chunks torn from his chest and were now on to something else—a herring or a clam.

What luck, Cole thought. To end up on an island with a stupid bear that didn't have brains enough to run away. And the seagulls? He hoped they choked to death. What pea brains, eating his ripped flesh as indifferently as they would bits of fish! They treated him like any other animal. Cole wanted to scream, "Hey, look at me! I'm Cole Matthews! I'm better than you." But all he could manage was a grunt. If only he had a gun.

The squawking of the gulls over the bay echoed like hollow laughter. They were laughing at him, Cole thought. He wished he had never come to this island. But he *was* here. Nothing could change that. He was trapped on a godforsaken island, alone, and mauled within an inch of his life by a white monster bear.

Cole tried to gather his wits. The mauling didn't make sense. In the past, everything had always been afraid of him. Why wasn't the bear scared? A bear with half a brain would have turned tail and run. Instead, this dumb animal had attacked. Now it wandered out in the woods somewhere, the mauling little more than an inconvenience to its morning.

Cole glanced down and spotted the knife blade lying by his side. It satisfied him to see the Spirit Bear's blood on the blade tip. Grimacing, he raised his left hand to wipe his own blood from his lips. He saw his fist tightly gripping the clump of white matted hair he had ripped off the bear. The sight of the hair caused him to shudder.

Cole tensed his arm to throw away the stark reminder of his mauling, but paused. Instead he worked his hand to his side and stuffed the hair in his pants pocket. If he lived through this, he would have something to brag about. He could prove he had fought a bear. The hair gave Cole a sense of power. No bear would willingly give up a big clump of hair.

Cole struggled to shift his position on the uneven ground, but stiffness had set into his joints like hardened cement. He couldn't roll to either side. If only he could use both arms. Struggling, he raised his head for a better look at his right arm. It lay mangled and useless. All he could see of his forearm was ripped shirt and ragged torn flesh. A bloody white bone jutted out near his elbow like a broken stick. His fingers looked artificial, pale and puffy from grabbing the Devil's Club. They faced the wrong direction. The only sensation he had from the arm was a throbbing burn in his shoulder.

The sight of his arm frightened Cole. He drew in a deep breath, but again pain stabbed at his chest, warning him. He returned to shallow tentative breaths, drawing air past his lips as if he were sipping from a straw.

Cole grimaced and struggled to raise his right knee, but he couldn't. The crushing bites to his thigh had rendered his leg lifeless. He relaxed his neck to catch his breath. Sweat stung his eyes.

And still it rained, cold rain, soaking into everything it touched. A breeze swayed the branches overhead. Cole's gaze wandered in a big circle around him. All of the landscape, the air, the trees, the animals, the water, the rain, all seemed to be part of something bigger. They moved in harmony, bending and flowing, twisting and breathing, as if connected. But Cole felt alone and apart. His soaked clothes chilled his bones. The hard ground pushed at his wounded body like a big hand shoving him away.

No, Cole thought, he was not a part of this place. He should not be here. It was not his choice to lie dying on a remote island, alone, unable to move. This place held him prisoner more securely than any jail cell. Here, he was powerless. He could not keep warm or find food.

His place was wearing dry clothes in a safe warm room, sleeping and eating without a care in the world. His place was having other people worry about him. His place was being in control. That was his place.

Haunting thoughts pried at Cole's mind. Night would come sooner or later, and with it, more rain and cold. What would happen when the last bit of warmth seeped from his body? What was death like? Did it hurt? Did it come fast like lightning from the sky or a blow from the Spirit Bear? Did death sneak around like a stinking seagull, trying to snatch life from a body like meat chunks from a rotting carcass? Or did life just flicker out like a dim candle?

Cole's tortured thoughts slowly gave way to an even worse possibility. What if death didn't happen right away? Would seagulls land on him and peck bits of warm meat from his body when he could no longer fight back? And where was the bear?

Waves of pain wracked Cole's body. With each agonizing wave, he bit at his lip and whimpered, trying not to cry out. All of his life he had been haunted by nightmares of helplessness. Some nights he dreamed he was drowning, unable to find the surface. Some nights he dreamed of fists raining down on him like giant hail. Worse yet were the dreams he had of being alone and no one caring about him. Now he was living his worst nightmare. Cole flopped his head to the side and spotted a small caterpillar inching over a rotted branch. He reached out his finger and crushed it. That would teach it not to crawl so close.

The sweet taste of blood kept seeping into Cole's mouth, forcing him to swallow. His stomach cramped. Wincing, he wiped at his mouth with his left hand, then stared at the glistening red on his knuckles. It reminded him of the bear's blood on the knife blade beside him. It also looked like the blood he had seen on the sidewalk after beating up Peter. The blood looked identical. This thought drifted about in his head but failed to gain meaning. Blood might look the same, but Peter was a loser and a jerk. Cole dropped his hand to the grass. The bear was a stupid lumbering moron.

Cole's stomach churned and cramped harder. A sour bile taste stung his throat. He dared not throw up, but he felt the urge coming like a freight train and he couldn't get off the tracks. Suddenly he convulsed and vomited. Instant pain attacked his chest, and the world swam in circles. Again and again the spasms came, and Cole flopped his head sideways to keep from choking. He tried to stop throwing up, but couldn't. Black patches danced across his vision, then he lost consciousness.

Hours later, Cole awoke feeling weak and confused. His thoughts drifted above him like restless air moving over the bay. The stink of vomit and the salty smell of rotting seaweed hung in the air, and overhead, a leaf drifted down in slow motion as if arriving from outer space.

Cole forced his head to the side and tried to focus. Vomit covered the ground beside his head. He could see chunks of the fish he had eaten. Beyond, he could see the mouth of the bay where the ocean disappeared into the dull, rain-misted sky.

Cole damned the rocks, the rain, and the endless ocean. What a fool he had been to come here instead of going to jail. At least in jail he would have been in the safety and comfort of a cell. He would have had some control. Here he was powerless, nobody to control, nobody to blame. Every action worked against him and hurt him.

A bitter loneliness swept over Cole as tears clouded his vision. He felt so small here, puked up on a remote forgotten shore and left to die. Was this how the world was going to get rid of him?

CHAPTER 9

A CONSTANT RAIN and shrouded gray sky masked the passing of hours, leaving Cole in a cruel time warp with only one possible end. He tried not to think about the end, but he could not ignore the maddening pain from his wounds.

As gusts of wind drove the chill deeper into his body, rain kept falling, penetrating his will, seeping into his consciousness, and flooding his soul. This rain fully intended to kill.

As Cole weakened, he stared up at the giant spruce tree towering above him. Desperate tears welled up inside and squeezed past his eyelids. The wind gusted harder.

What did it matter anymore if he died? Nobody else cared about him, so why should he care about himself? As Cole's gaze drifted among the branches of the tree, a small bird's nest tucked into the fork of two branches caught his attention. The nest rested near the trunk, protected from both the wind and the rain. As Cole watched, a small gray sparrow landed in the nest, twitched about with a flurry of activity, then flew off. Soon it returned again.

Each time the sparrow returned, it carried a bug or a worm in its beak and busied itself over the nest. The visits brought faint chirping sounds. Cole squinted and made out little heads jutting above the nest. This was a mother bird feeding her young. Up there on a branch, barely spitting distance away, little sparrows rested dry and warm, having food brought to them in the comfort of a nest built by their mother.

The sight of the baby birds irritated Cole. Without his injuries, he could easily have crawled up and knocked the nest down. That's what the stupid birds deserved.

After feeding, the mother flitted to a branch near the nest. She ruffled her wings and chest feathers, keeping an eye on her young. Watching the bird made Cole curse every second of his miserable and haphazard life. If he were the mother bird, he would just leave the babies to fend for themselves. She didn't owe them anything.

That's how Cole felt—he didn't owe anyone anything. Nobody had ever cared for him, so why should he care about anyone else? He wouldn't even be here on this island, injured, if it weren't for other people and their lame ideas. Nothing had been his fault. Cole's bitterness flickered to life once more. His anger helped to focus his thoughts, but it could not stop the frigid drizzle or the torturing pain that wracked his body. Nor could it ward off the loneliness.

The wind that tugged at Cole's tattered clothing seemed distant. As his attention drifted and his senses dulled, rain numbed his face. Cole stared blankly at the thin sliver of blue sky on the western horizon. Exhaustion finally dragged him into a stuporous sleep.

Unconscious, he dreamed of the colorful at.óow blanket. His left hand twitched and moved back and forth, pretending to pull the at.óow over his freezing body. The imaginary blanket shielded him from the cold as it had protected many generations before him. Under the imaginary blanket, he slept soundly.

A loud rumble woke Cole from his sleep. At first he thought he had gone blind. Then slowly he realized it was nighttime. The wind had let up, but the cold rain still fell relentlessly from some endless reservoir in the sky. Then a blinding flash of lightning lit the horizon. Seconds later, deep rumbling thunder rolled overhead, followed by another flash of lightning.

Before the light collapsed back into darkness, Cole realized the at.óow he had dreamed of was not covering him. And he sensed a presence. He peered wide-eyed into the black night but could see nothing. Then lightning flashed again with a sharp crack, closer this time. In that instant, Cole saw it, ghostlike. Barely fifty feet away, the giant Spirit Bear stood motionless in the rain.

Then the night went black again.

Terrified, Cole waited, his eyes prying at the darkness. Had the bear returned to kill him? As he waited, the storm worsened. The wind picked up, gusting harder. Rain fell in torrents, and thunder rumbled across the sky like empty barrels rolling toward the horizon. When the next bolt of lightning lit the bay, Cole searched frantically.

Nothing! Gone! Again the Spirit Bear had vanished.

Cole grimaced. He hated this bear. What a coward. This creature was waiting until he grew so weak he couldn't fight back. Then it would finish him off. Cole moaned as a violent gust of wind pummeled his body. Would the bear just kill him and leave him to the seagulls, or would it eat him?

Lightning flashed closer, stabbing down with long, probing fingers. The rumbling thunder started crashing and exploding. To protect himself, Cole tried to curl into a ball, but pain stung at his chest, lungs, and useless hip, and he cried out, "Help me! Somebody help me!" The black night and the wind drowned out his voice. Now the lightning flashed so often that the sky stayed lit for several long seconds at a time and the thunder came in a continuous roar. Trees swayed and bent with the wind. White-capped waves frothed and churned in the bay.

Cole pinched his eyes closed against the piercing rain. Suddenly a prickling sensation, as if ants were swarming over him, covered his whole body. A searing light flashed, and a deafening explosion detonated beside him. He heard a cracking sound as the sky crashed to earth with a violent impact that shook the ground. Splinters of branches rained down. Then came silence and calm, as if the impact had paralyzed the sky. The rain and wind paused, and an acrid smell like burning wire filled the air.

Cole lay frozen by fear. A sobering power had attacked the earth. This power made the bear's attack seem gentle. "No more! No more!" he moaned. "Please, no more!"

But there was more. The storm raged on as Cole lay trembling, his eyes frantic. The explosion had shocked his mind awake. Never in his life had he felt so exposed, so vulnerable, so helpless. He had no control. To this storm, he was as insignificant as a leaf. Cole blinked in stunned realization. He had always been this weak. How could he have ever thought he truly controlled anything?

The acid electrical smell burned his nose and mixed with the smell of wet vomit on the ground. Cole swallowed hard to keep from throwing up again as the storm kept attacking the sky and earth around him.

Finally the wind lost its fury, and the sky ran out of rain. The thunder subsided, rumbling back and forth across the sky, searching for someplace else to go. Cole swallowed the taste of bile in his throat and listened to the rumbling overhead. Then once more he lost consciousness.

When he awoke next, the rain had stopped. Vaguely, he could make out the big spruce tree lying on the ground only feet away from where he lay. Moment by moment, he sorted out what had happened during the storm. Lightning had struck the tree. The splitting sound, the thunderous impact, the splintering and bits of branches showering him, all had happened when the huge tree crashed to earth.

Cole gazed up at the night sky. A bright full moon drifted ghostlike among the broken clouds. The tortured air had calmed but still shifted back and forth. Cole felt desperately weak. Fighting to survive, he could stay here a short while longer.

Giving up, he could pass quickly over the edge. Which way did he want to go? He clenched his teeth against the pain and despair. Which way did he want to go?

Cole focused his blurred vision on the full moon. It helped him to remain on this side. As he stared, he puzzled at the moon's shape. Something in that hazy shape held meaning. Edwin had said something about a circle. So had Garvey. What had they said? Cole could not remember, but he kept staring up.

Later, Cole flopped his head to the side. He could make out the bay and see moonlight reflecting against one shore. The shoreline faded into darkness in the shadow of the trees. Seeing no sign of the Spirit Bear, Cole returned his attention to the fallen tree beside him.

That was when he remembered the baby sparrows. He tried to make out where they might be now among the fallen and twisted branches. He squinted harder, but all he saw was black. What had happened to the baby birds?

Mustering all his strength, he raised his head, and with a weak and pinched voice he called into the darkened branches, "Are you okay?"

CHAPTER 10

As Cole lay thinking about the sparrows, pain surged back and forth through his body. He felt himself slipping into darkness and blinked hard, doggedly clinging to life, willing himself to not let go. For hours he kept blinking, but by dawn, staying conscious seemed less important. Now he hung on the edge of existence, detached from the real world, weightless and moved by the wind. Thoughts of the sparrows disappeared.

As daylight seeped through thick curtains of haze, a new pain arrived and gradually worsened until it could not be ignored. Pressure had built in his lower gut. He needed desperately to go to the bathroom but held back, grimacing. He had no way to squirm away from his own waste. Finally the pain became so sharp, Cole let out a deep groan. He couldn't fight his own body any longer.

Painful shame gripped Cole as waste slipped from his body and a raw stench filled the air. He jerked his head and arm to drive away the mosquitoes swarming around him, but they returned instantly. Finally he gave up. An absolute and utter hopelessness overwhelmed him. He felt like a helpless baby, not able to roll away from his own filth. He wanted to hate somebody, to be angry, and to place blame on everything and everyone for this moment. But anger took energy, and Cole no longer had energy.

As the sun climbed over the trees, black horse flies started attacking. Unable to drive them away, Cole felt the huge insects bite him. He gazed desperately away at the fallen tree beside him. A ten-foot trunk remained upright, its ragged top charred where lightning had struck. Whiffs of smoke still curled upward. Beside the trunk lay a tangle of broken timber.

Cole watched the birds flitting among the downed branches, feeding on bugs and worms. For them the storm was over and life continued. The falling of the tree was simply a natural reality, like the passing of another day. Cole eyed the birds as he struggled to concentrate. Something in those branches had been important. His gaze wandered to the ripped-up grass under the splintered branches and crushed boughs. What had been so important in that maze of destruction? He spotted a small, brown, fist-sized clump of twigs not ten feet away.

The nest.

That was it! That was what he had been search-ing for. Something about that nest was important. But what?

And then he found them.

First one, then two, then a third and fourth— four lifeless baby sparrows, scattered in the short grass where they had been thrown from their nest. Matted fuzz covered the twisted little bodies. Two had died with their big yellow beaks open as if searching for food. The other two lay facing the nest, their necks reaching out. Even in death, the sparrows had strained toward their nest. They had tried to make it back to the safety of their home.

Cole envied the dead sparrows. He had never really known any home. It sure wasn't the big brick building that his parents landscaped and fixed up to impress the neighbors. Nor was it the empty space he returned to most days after school. Even before his parents' divorce, Cole had always wanted to run away from that place.

As Cole stared at the tiny bodies, sadness flooded through him. The sparrows were so frail, helpless, and innocent. They hadn't deserved to die. Then again, what right did they have to live? This haunted Cole. Did the birds' insignificant little existences have any meaning at all? Or did his?

He watched one solitary gray sparrow hopping among the broken branches near the nest. Was that the mother? Was she looking for her young? Cole licked his cracked and dried lips. At least the babies had a mother to search for them. Nobody, not even a scrawny gray bird, was looking for him.

Cole's eyes grew moist. He couldn't stop thinking about the tiny birds strewn in the grass. Had they suffered before they died? Or did their fragile existence just suddenly stop? And what had happened to their energy when their hearts quit beating? It didn't seem right that now maggots would eat the bodies. Or maybe they would just rot into the ground to help the grass grow. Maybe that was the circle Edwin had spoken of. You live, die, and rot, then something else lives, dies, and rots.

Cole understood this cycle. Beside him a tree had died. Already, ants and bugs crawled among the cracked bark and splintered wood. For them life went on. In a few weeks they would make new homes from the wood. With time, the tree would rot and become dirt. Then a new seed would fall and grow, and another tree would push upward. Years later, that tree would fall back to earth and begin the cycle all over again.

Yes, death was part of living. Cole knew his

own body would eventually die and decay and be reduced to dirt. That was okay. That was how the world worked. But how had the world benefited from his living? Was he no better than a tree or some weed? Was his life just fertilizer for the soil?

Cole grunted angrily—he didn't want to die yet. Yes, someday that would be part of his circle. Someday he would lie in his own waste and be eaten by maggots. But not now! Suddenly, in that moment, Cole made a simple decision.

He wanted to live.

In death there was no control, no anger, no one to blame, no choices, no nothing. To be alive was to have choice. The power to choose was real power, not the fake power of making others afraid. Cole knew he had used that fake power many times. All of his life he had squandered his choices, wallowing in revenge and self-pity, keeping himself down. Now, as he lay near death, those he had hated were safe and warm. Those he had blamed were still alive and well. He had hurt himself most. Life was empty and meaningless unless he found some meaning.

Maybe it was a vision or maybe just a thought. Maybe a hallucination. A simple image entered Cole's mind: a tiny sparrow in a nest, helpless, neck straining upward, mouth gaping open. The sparrow Cole imagined was not angry.

The young bird was helpless. It knew nothing of pride or control. It pleaded only for help, wanting nothing more than a worm brought by its mother. A worm was food, food was energy, and energy was life. The baby begged simply for life.

Mosquitoes and horseflies swarmed around Cole's face. He grunted and jerked his head. It didn't matter who was at fault for his dismal life. All that mattered was living. Cole wanted to live and once again make choices. But to live he needed food. And soon!

But how? Every ounce of food he had eaten earlier lay in vomited chunks beside his body.

Cole fingered blades of grass under his left hand, then broke off a few and brought them to his lips. His dry, swollen tongue felt stuffed into his mouth. Deliberately, he opened his crusted lips and poked the grass inside. As he worked his jaws to chew, he reached for more grass.

Gradually the stringy green blades formed a wad in his mouth, and he swallowed. Without water, the clump caught in his throat. Again he tried to swallow, but gagged. The clump was stuck and refused to go down or come back up.

Panicking, Cole stifled a cough—he didn't dare cough. Frantically he gagged harder, twisting his head, straining until he felt blood vessels bulge on his face. He couldn't breathe. The clump was suffocating him. Raising his head, mouth wide open, he convulsed, frantic and desperate to dislodge the grass. His body screamed for air. Then suddenly, explosively, he coughed, ejecting the wad of grass.

Violent pain, like the claws of the Spirit Bear, ripped at his ribs. Cole gasped and clenched his teeth, hugging his side with his left arm while his head swam in a fog. A long grueling minute passed before the pain eased and he dared allow a shallow breath to seep past his lips.

Sweat beaded his forehead. When he opened his eyes again, he glanced around and found the stringy lump of grass on the ground beside his chest. He stared. What other choice did he have if he wanted to live? Reluctantly he picked up the wad and returned it to his mouth. This time he chewed a very long time before swallowing. He exhaled with relief when the grass went down.

As Cole reached for more grass, he spotted a worm near his hand and grabbed it instead. The long worm bunched up and squirmed to get free, so he brought it quickly to his mouth and poked it safely past his cracked lips. It coiled against his tongue as he bit it and started chewing. The worm was easier to chew than grass and went down with the first swallow. Cole searched for another. As he searched, the rain began again. He opened his mouth and let the drops tickle his tongue. Maybe the rain would bring out more worms.

The second and third worms Cole found were smaller, and he ate them quickly. His teeth crunched on dirt, and there wasn't much flavor, but he chewed as he watched another big worm creep slowly past his hand just inches beyond his reach. Failing to find more worms, he turned his attention to bugs. The ground teemed with insects, and he began putting ants, beetles, spiders, and even a fuzzy caterpillar into his mouth. With each insect, he closed his eyes and imagined a baby sparrow reaching upward with an opened beak.

Finally, exhausted, Cole rested. Sometime later, the rain stopped, and a warm sun brought back the thick clouds of mosquitoes and horse-flies. They swarmed over Cole's body as if it were a dead carcass. He tried to shoo them away with an awkward swing of his hand, but they returned before his fingers touched the ground. Dozens blanketed his bloody face, neck, chest, and arms.

The only place Cole felt no bites was on his broken right arm. He raised his head to look. His right arm was shaded black with mosquitoes, as thick as hair. Cole could only stare, and finally he closed his eyes. In the darkness, he still felt the sharp bites of the horseflies, and he felt the mosquitoes, dozens and dozens of tiny pins pricking him, sucking at him, leaving their itchy venom behind. If only he had the at.óow blanket for protection. He had no idea where the blanket was. How could he have ever tried to burn it? It would have protected him from the cold, the rain, the wind, and the insects. It might even have protected him from himself.

Cole lost consciousness again.

Hours later, drifting awake, Cole became aware of a tickling sensation on his left arm. He opened his eyes to find a small gray mouse perched on his elbow, working its way toward his wrist. It stopped every step to poke a whiskered nose about. Cole lay motionless as the skittish mouse ventured across his forearm and sniffed at his wrist, then inched onto his upturned palm. Cole held his breath. He would have only one chance. Catching this mouse would be better than a dozen worms or a hundred bugs.

The mosquitoes had not slowed their feasting. Hundreds covered Cole's exposed skin, their tiny torsos swollen with blood. Several landed on his eyelids, and Cole blinked to drive them away—he dared not move his hand to swat at them. Focusing his gaze on the mouse, he waited for it to take one more step. It moved its whiskered head back and forth with jerky caution, then stepped forward.

Cole clamped his hand closed.

CHAPTER 11

THE MOUSE STRUGGLED, biting at Cole's fingers with razor-sharp teeth, its tiny feet clawing frantically to escape. Cole pitied the scared little mouse, but he held on, gripping with all his strength. This mouse was his quarry, like a gull catching a herring or an owl catching a rabbit. He squeezed the mouse but was too weak to stop the struggling.

Cole felt the mouse squirming free, so quickly he brought his fist to his mouth. He pressed his hand against his lips and forced the struggling rodent between his teeth. It kept struggling, biting at Cole's lips and tongue.

Cole bit down, too, and a tiny bone crunched. The mouse spasmed but kept squirming. Cole bit again but his jaw lacked strength. Still the mouse wiggled and twisted, frantically chewing at Cole's tongue. For a brief second, Cole felt a furry head pass between his back teeth and he willed his jaws together with every ounce of strength he could gather. The small skull crushed, and then the mouse stiffened and quit squirming.

With the dead mouse bunched in his cheek, Cole rested his jaw. Occasionally the tiny body twitched. Gradually, Cole worked his teeth together, gnawing on the body. Salty fluids filled his mouth, and he forced himself to again imagine a baby sparrow with an opened beak. Food was energy, and energy was life.

Eating the mouse exhausted Cole, and by the time he had chewed up the tiny bones and swallowed the wad of tough furry skin, he lay spent, mouth gaping open. His jaw ached and felt hollow. Mosquitoes landed on his lips and tongue at will. His skin had become swollen and puffy, burning with a fiery itch.

Cole wanted desperately to live, but how? The wretched insects sucked life from him faster than he could replenish it. He closed his eyes to the bloodletting, but that did not stop the torment. In the maddening darkness he sensed another movement. Again he opened his eyes, half expecting to see the Spirit Bear. Instead, he found two seagulls near his head, pecking fish chunks from the vomit he had thrown up in the grass.

My puke, Cole thought. They're eating my puke.

In that moment, Cole realized how badly he wanted to live. The food he had thrown up was still food. Those fish bits still contained energy, and energy was life. No thieving seagull was going to steal life from him. He jerked his arm at the gulls. "Mine," he grunted. "That's mine." Squawking, the gulls hopped beyond his reach.

Cole stretched his arm out, picked a small chunk of fish from the grass, and brought it to his mouth. After swallowing, he reached for more. Bit by bit he ate until the few remaining pieces were too small to pinch between his fingers. Finally he relaxed. Eating had taken his last ounce of energy. He closed his eyes as drizzle fell again. The falling moisture felt like more mosquitoes landing, but as it turned to rain, it cooled Cole's burning skin. He opened his cracked lips and let rain hit his swollen, chalky tongue.

Earlier, Cole had felt hollow and weak, as if all the blood had emptied from his body. Now he felt something difficult to describe. Despite the cold, energy seeped through his body, letting him grasp thoughts and hold them in his mind. He felt satisfaction. He had provided for himself and could feel his body absorbing the food he had eaten. But still his body desperately needed water. He was thirsty. So very thirsty.

As the rain fell again, the ground softened.

Cole dug with his fingers and brought mud up to smear onto his swollen neck and face. He smeared mud over his broken arm and onto his ripped-open chest. Maybe this would help keep the mosquitoes away. The wet dirt soothed Cole's burning skin. When his arm tired, he rested again.

Gradually, rain pooled where he had dug up mud beside him. He stared at the muddy water, then placed his hand into the puddle. Each movement was forced as he cupped his palm and brought the brown murky liquid up to his mouth. Again and again, he reached for more water. Sometimes only a few drops made it past his dried lips, but gradually moisture coated his throat and finally allowed him to swallow.

Cole let his weary arm collapse to the ground. Resting, he gazed out toward the bay at the eagles snatching fish from the surface. Nearer the shore swam a mother seal with her pups, their heads bobbing in the water as they worked the fish schools near the rocks. Cole scanned the ground once more and caught two more worms that surfaced with the new rain. He dropped them into his mouth, and chewed. The animals weren't the only ones who could forage to survive.

The sound of a twig breaking was Cole's only warning. He turned his head to find the Spirit

Bear standing barely twenty feet away, staring at him, one paw forward as if frozen in midstride. The bear's shiny nose twitched as raindrops beaded into splashed pearls on its shaggy hair. Its eyes glinted and flickered.

Cole's heart raced, and his wounds throbbed. He felt the ripping of his skin all over again and heard once more the breaking of his bones. Too numb with cold and fear to even cry out, he eyed the Spirit Bear standing like a carved statue.

Cole licked at his cracked lips. Had the bear returned to kill him, or was it just toying with him? He found himself trembling with fear, not of death, but of helplessness. He hated being at the mercy of the world around him. Why didn't this monstrous white creature just walk in and finish what it had started? A single bite from its massive jaw, one hard swat from its powerful paw, anything now would tip the balance and end this nightmare.

One way or another, Cole decided to bring this moment to a conclusion. His mouth held little moisture, but deliberately he dredged up spit from deep in his throat, all the while meeting the bear's intense gaze with one of his own.

When not one more drop of moisture would form, Cole painfully lifted his head. He sucked in the deepest breath he dared. He was spitting at more than the Spirit Bear. He was spitting at his life. The world would take him to the grave with a slimy goober on its face. Cole Matthews would still have the last word.

Preparing for his final act of defiance, Cole drew his chin back, then he spit hard, flinging the saliva with a desperate throw of his head. Pain attacked him from all sides, but he kept his eyes open. He wanted the satisfaction of watching this last moment.

As if in slow motion, the glob of spit arched weakly toward the Spirit Bear but landed in the grass far short of its mark. Cole collapsed. That was it then, he had done all he could. Now the world could do as it pleased with him.

The Spirit Bear raised its head slightly and sniffed the air with a long curious breath, then it started forward. Cole tensed. This was how the first attack should have ended.

CHAPTER 12

THE SPIRIT BEAR approached Cole with a slow lazy stride, its head held low. Cole clenched his fist. Maybe he could hold up his arm. Maybe he had energy for one last swing.

Ten feet away, the bear paused where Cole's spit had hit the grass. It lowered its head and sniffed. Still eyeing Cole, the Spirit Bear casually licked up the spit, raised its head, eyes mild and curious, then turned and sauntered away.

Cole felt a sudden rush of tears and emotion. Death would be okay if it came fast, existence ending in one last violent moment of defiance. Cole could understand that kind of death. But here, he lay exposed, alone, ignored, his life leaking from his body like water from some rusty bucket. Even a bear considered him insignificant, licking up his spit as casually as if it were dew.

The Spirit Bear never once slowed or looked back. Cole fought back his tears until the last trace of white faded into the thick underbrush, and then he began to sob. He was dying, alone and insignificant, and nobody cared.

Drifting off into a dream world, Cole imagined he was a baby bird in a nest. Around him, a storm raged and the trees swayed violently. Driving rain pelted him like hail.

Frantic, Cole struggled to fly, but he couldn't escape the nest. All he could do was open his beak wide and raise it upward toward the sky, the action a simple admission that he was powerless. There were no conditions, no vices, no lies, no deceit, no manipulation. Only submission and a simple desire to live. He wanted to live, but for that he needed help; otherwise his life would end in the nest.

Suddenly, the violent winds calmed, and the rain stopped. Cole strained upward with his opened beak as his senses drifted back into the real world of pain. Again he was in his wounded body on an island prison. The storm had stopped, and something had awakened him. An overpowering animal smell. His eyes opened.

Looming over Cole, its breath warm and musty, towered the Spirit Bear. Inches away. Its legs rose like pillars beside Cole's arms, and mist glistened on its white hair.

The world stopped.

For Cole there was no wind, no cold, no time,

no pain, no sound. There existed only one object, the Spirit Bear. Its shiny black eyes held eternity. Its intense gaze penetrated, never wavering.

Surprisingly, Cole did not feel the terror he had once known. Maybe the Spirit Bear had come to kill him. Maybe it was only curious. Whatever the reason, Cole gazed calmly back up at the bear. He knew he would fight to the last moment to live. Any animal would do that. Even worms coiled back and forth to escape capture and death. But Cole also knew that if he died, his time had arrived. It would be like the baby birds, or like the worms, or the mouse. It was his turn.

Cole's eyes watered, and he blinked. This was the end, then. Resigned to his fate, he gazed into the bear's eyes but found no aggression—only curiosity. It was as if the bear were waiting. But waiting for what? Instinctively, Cole gathered what little spit he could in his mouth. When the meager fluid bathed his tongue, he stopped, paused, and then swallowed.

Cole did not understand why he had swallowed or what happened next. Hesitantly he raised his left hand off the ground. As if reaching for an electric fence, he cautiously extended his fingers toward the Spirit Bear's shoulder. Inches away, he paused.

Awareness flickered in the bear's eyes.

Cole forced his hand forward until his fingers touched the bear's moist white coat. If he was going to die, he wanted to know what the animal felt like that killed him.

Still the bear remained motionless.

Cole's fingers sank into the bushy white hair until he touched solid body. With his fingertips, he felt warmth. He felt the bear's breath and heartbeat. And he felt one more thing. He felt trust. But why? Already he had tried to kill the bear. He had spit at it. This bear had defied him, and he had hated it with every fiber of his existence. Still touching the bear, Cole paused. Then he drew his hand away.

The Spirit Bear never blinked, never twitched a muscle. Only when Cole's hand again rested on the ground, only then did the towering animal lower its huge head as if nodding. A second time it dipped its head, then stepped back away. With one fluid motion, it swung around and ambled silently down toward the waterline.

Cole watched, forgetting to breathe. He expected the bear to stop when it reached the shoreline, but the great white animal waded into the water and swam with powerful strokes out into the bay toward the open ocean. A thin wake spread like a giant V behind the departing creature until it became a silhouetted speck, finally disappearing. Cole let his imagination keep the bear visible awhile longer. Finally, even that image faded.

Cole blinked and took a breath, as if he were awakening.

Around him, the land had come alive. A clear horizon showed under a dark blanket of clouds. Reflections of blue and gray swirled on the water as a fresh breeze ruffled the spruce boughs and sent ripples along the shoreline. Seagulls screeched and squawked their way out over the bay, diving and hunting for food. Barely a hundred feet away, the mother seal and her spotted pups appeared, their doglike heads peeking out of the water.

The air still carried the rotten smells of vomit and death, but also the fresh odor of seaweed and moss and cedar and salt. Vivid colors glistened wet in the bright light.

A strange thought occurred to Cole: the world was beautiful. Yes, the world *was* beautiful! Even the wet moss and crushed grass near his hand was beautiful. Staring at the delicate patterns, he wondered why he had never noticed this all before. How much beauty had he missed in his lifetime? How much beauty had he destroyed?

But the past was another time and another life that Cole could never recapture—and didn't want to. He knew only the moment, and this moment he was alive, the most alive he had ever felt. It struck Cole as odd that he should feel this way at the very moment when his body had reached the point at which it could no longer exist. Even as he stared at the moss, deep inside him the balance was shifting to the other side. Clinging to life was like hanging from a bar on the playground at school. On the playground he could hold on for a long time, but when his grip finally tired, his fingers slipped quickly and he fell.

Now Cole felt himself slipping fast. He had struggled too long to hold on, his energy bleeding away. Now it was his turn to die. This thought made Cole sad, but he accepted it. He felt content. Before the end of life he had seen beauty. He had trusted and been trusted.

That was enough.

Cole's head rested on a patch of spongy moss that acted as a pillow. His pain seemed to float, like a haze, outside his body. He closed his eyes, relaxed, and let the balance shift. And as it shifted, Cole felt himself floating upward into a cloud. Gradually a buzzing sound gathered in his head, growing louder and louder. The sound bothered Cole. He wanted quiet now.

Abruptly the buzzing stopped and squawking seagulls surrounded his body. He could hear them arguing over him. This was what it felt like to die. He hadn't imagined it being so noisy. The seagulls began pecking at his arms and legs. Cole could not open his eyes, but he jerked his arm. Why couldn't the seagulls leave him alone? Why couldn't they wait just a little longer until he had died? Did they have to pick meat off his bones while he was still breathing?

Instead of stopping, the pecking grew worse. Now the gulls were pulling at his legs and shoulders with giant beaks, trying to lift him. Bizarre sensations bombarded Cole as his body was dragged and bumped across the rocks. Sharp pain stabbed through his wounds. Then the loud cry of the seagulls turned into garbled gibberish as they tugged at his shirt and shoes. What were they doing to him?

Gradually, soft and warm sensations enveloped Cole, like being wrapped in a blanket. His head was tilted forward, and warm liquid filled his mouth. It didn't make sense. How could rain be warm? His head must be in a puddle with muddy water running past his lips. Or maybe it was blood. He spit out the liquid, and felt it warm on his neck. He didn't want to drown in blood or muddy water. But again warm liquid flowed past his lips, and Cole gave in. It didn't matter anymore how he died. He could drown, freeze, or be pecked apart by seagulls. All that mattered was that the balance had changed, and now he was drifting over the edge.

"Hang in there, Champ! Hang in there!" a voice sounded.

The buzzing sounded again, louder, deafening, like a swarm of giant bees preparing to attack. Then the world tilted and bounced. With each bounce, pain throbbed in Cole's chest. Something cradled his neck and steadied his head when the jarring grew too intense. He kept trying to push himself over the edge, but again his head was lifted and more warm fluid flowed past his lips.

"Hang with me, Champ!"

Cole spit out another mouthful. The sweet fluid was keeping his pain alive, allowing all the bouncing and the noise to continue. But nothing could stop it from leaking past his teeth and swollen parched tongue. The warm fluid flowed down into his throat and brought back the cold. Chills wracked his body in uncontrolled spasms. He moaned. When would this horrible nightmare ever end?

Then, suddenly, he awoke.

His eyes opened.

And nothing made sense.

Gone were the bay and the fallen tree. A dark and restless sky still moved overhead, but where was the hard ground, the wet, the mud, the dead birds? A thick blanket held both of his arms in close to his chest. The blanket was brown and not the colorful at.óow. Where was the at.óow?

Cole's vision was blurred, but he understood that he was lying in the bottom of a shallow aluminum skiff. Kneeling on one knee, steering, was Edwin, the Tlingit elder who had helped bring him out to the island. Instead of his normal detached faraway look, Edwin's eyebrows furrowed with concern.

Cole blinked hard to focus. His head rested on someone's lap. Then he recognized Garvey, leaning over him, his face haggard with worry. "We'll be home soon!" Garvey shouted above the roar of the engine.

Too weak to answer, Cole let his eyes close again. He struggled to recall what had happened but couldn't.

Garvey shouted something to Edwin, and the engine revved louder. Spray whipped across the bow as the boat surged into the waves. Cole held his breath and tensed to lessen the pain in his ribs. It was as if somebody were beating on his chest with a bat. He felt Garvey's strong grip tighten each time they hit a big wave.

The hard bucking lasted forever, and Cole was drunk with pain by the time the boat finally slowed. The screaming of the engine grew muted, replaced by anxious voices shouting to them. Garvey and Edwin shouted back. Then the boat bumped against something.

Cole opened his eyes. They had pulled alongside a dock. A cluster of people crowded next to the boat, staring down at him. People were moving, reaching, shouting. Cole cried out in pain as he was lifted from the boat. His ribs and leg felt as if they were being ripped from his body. Someone slipped, and Cole's leg scraped against the edge of the dock. He heard himself cry out. More footsteps pounded and voices shouted. The dock swayed, and Cole grabbed blindly at the air to stop the world from moving. He couldn't take any more of this torture. It had become violent.

The commotion continued. Tilting dangerously back and forth, Cole felt himself lifted onto a stretcher and carried up the dock to a waiting van. Doors slammed, a motor revved, and there was more bouncing as the van raced down the road. Cole's pain faded into delirium.

The next sensation was of entering a room and being lifted onto a soft warm bed. Careful hands dried him and worked his pants off. He dreamed that the Spirit Bear was ripping at his leg. But instead of a growl, a woman's soft voice said, "Easy, easy—you'll be okay. Just relax." Cole's uncontrollable shivers were replaced by hot sweating as a towel patted his forehead.

When the commotion finally stopped, Cole lay completely spent, drifting in and out of consciousness. He felt a warm blanket being tucked in around his neck, and he opened his eyes. Where was the at.óow?

Seeing Cole's eyes open, Edwin and Garvey stepped forward, one on each side of his bed. Edwin studied Cole. "Sure busted yourself up," he said plainly.

Garvey nodded agreement. "Lightning knocked down a big tree. The branches must have hit you."

Cole tried to speak, but no words came to his throat.

A short round–faced Tlingit woman crowded in beside the bed. "His wounds aren't from any tree," she said, pulling back the blanket. "Look."

Edwin glanced down at the bloody red gashes surrounded by puffy ashen skin and whistled low. "Those are bite and claw wounds."

The woman nodded. "He's been attacked by a bear."

Cole nodded.

Fear flashed in Garvey's eyes.

"I'm okay," Cole succeeded in grunting weakly.

A thin smile failed to hide Garvey's concern. "Half your bones are busted, your body is swollen like one huge mosquito bite, and you're nearly starved to death. Believe me, Champ, you're not okay."

Cole forced a nod. "I *am* okay," he grunted again.

CHAPTER 13

A SHORT, SQUAT man poked his head inside Cole's room. "Ketchikan can't send a medivac plane until morning," he called out. "It's getting dark and weather has set in."

The nurse felt Cole's forehead. "Looks like you'll be spending the night at Rosey's one-star hotel."

Edwin nodded at Cole. "If you hadn't guessed, this is Rosey." A rare smile creased his lips. "She's the best nurse in Drake."

"The only nurse," Rosey added.

"If you live through Rosey," Edwin said, "you'll live through anything."

Cole shuddered with another spasm of chills as Rosey gave Edwin a light shove. "You and Garvey go make yourselves useful," she said. "Get another blanket."

Garvey handed Rosey the at.óow blanket off a chair beside the bed. "Here, we brought this in from the island."

"It's damp," she said. "Grab a fresh one from the closet."

When Cole spotted the colorful blanket beside him, he felt a sudden warmth. He reached out and grabbed its edge.

Garvey studied Cole, letting him clutch the wet at.óow as Edwin brought another blanket. He squeezed Cole's shoulder. "We'll talk more later. Get some rest now."

Cole let go of the at.óow and gripped Garvey's arm.

"I'm not going anywhere," Garvey reassured him. "Rosey and I will be here all night with you."

"Thanks," Cole whispered.

Rosey pushed in beside the bed. "This might sting a little." She poked a needle into Cole's left arm. "I'm starting an IV drip to get some fluids and antibiotics into you." Finishing, she tilted Cole's head up and put some pills gently inside his mouth. "Now, take these tablets. They should help the pain."

Cole sipped water from the glass she held to his lips and struggled to swallow the pills. When they finally went down, Rosey began working on Cole's wounds. The door opened, and another Tlingit woman brought in a Thermos of hot soup and set it next to the bed. Rosey turned to

Garvey. "Maybe you can get some food into this guy."

Edwin remained standing along the wall, watching intently as Garvey placed a big pillow under Cole's head and ladled spoonfuls of chicken broth between his cracked lips.

Cole's pain dulled as the medication took effect. Sipping soup, he watched Rosey. She worked cheerfully, as if there were nothing in the world she would rather be doing. When she left the room for more dressings, Garvey turned to Cole. "That bear used you for a chew toy." He pursed his lips with concern. "I'm sorry for getting you into this."

Cole had many things he wanted to explain but he was too weak and tired now. He shook his head. "My fault!" he whispered.

Garvey glanced at Edwin, who kept his focused gaze. Rosey returned to the bed, her hands filled with rolls of gauze and a brown plastic bottle. Garvey moved away from the bed to give her room. "You get some rest while Rosey finishes patching you up," he said to Cole.

"Can't do much patching," Rosey said. "He has broken bones. I wish we had him in a hospital tonight."

Cole closed his eyes while Rosey cleaned and bandaged his open wounds. The medicine made him sleepy.

Finishing her work, Rosey whispered to Garvey, "That bear had quite a time with him. He has broken ribs and maybe a broken pelvis. Add to that hypothermia and a broken leg and arm. I'm surprised he's even talking. Must be a tough kid."

"Not as tough as he thinks," Garvey whispered back.

Edwin murmured, "He'll be okay if he ever finds a reason to live."

Cole heard everyone's words as he drifted off.

He slept troubled, dreaming of people he knew coming toward him out of a misty haze. Each person helped him. Garvey fed him. Rosey fixed his wounds. His father gave him money. Edwin offered him advice. His mother cleaned him and handed him new clothes.

Cole liked being helped. He liked using people. Suddenly a bolt of lightning struck, and all the people turned into monsters. Everything they had done for Cole faded, and they laughed at him. "You fool!" they called. "Why should we do anything for you? You're nothing! You're a baby-faced con!"

Cole awoke in a sweat. It was night. He searched the darkness frantically. He heard regular breaths near him in the dark. "Garvey," he called, realizing he could talk. "Garvey."

Garvey's hoarse voice answered, "You okay, Cole?"

Cole heard someone getting up to snap the lights on. Garvey, still wearing his rumpled jeans and faded wool shirt, hurried to his bedside. A door opened from the next room, and Rosey rushed in. "What's wrong?" she asked.

Cole looked at the two of them, his nightmare still haunting him. "I had a dream," he said, his voice raspy. "People helped me, then they turned into monsters and laughed at me."

"It was just a dream," Garvey said, resting his hand on Cole's arm.

"But you two were there."

Rosey took Cole's hand in hers. "Well, I'm not a monster." She smiled. "Maybe Garvey is."

Cole didn't smile. "Why do you guys help me?"

Rosey looked at her watch. "It sure isn't for the pay and good hours." Then she shrugged. "Why live if you can't help others and make the world a better place?"

Cole looked up at Garvey. "Why do *you* help me?"

"Because we're friends."

Cole let his frustration show. "No. You didn't even know me when you first started helping me in Minneapolis."

Garvey studied Cole before answering. "You're right. I did it for myself."

Cole nodded. "That's what I figured—you didn't care about me. You were—"

"You're wrong," Garvey said. "I did care about you. But helping others is how I help myself."

"You need help?" Cole asked, surprised.

Garvey nodded. "I see a lot of myself in you. When I was your age, I spent five long years in prison for things I'll go to my grave regretting. I lived my early years here in Drake, but no one cared enough to take me through Circle Justice. If they had, maybe things would have been different." He shook his head with a sad smile. "Take my word for it, jail scars the soul. And I was never able to help those I hurt."

"Cole," Rosey said, touching his bandaged arm. "In a few months your body will heal, but time won't heal your mind as easily. Helping others can help heal your wounds of the spirit."

Still troubled by his dream, Cole said, "There are people who want to hurt me."

Rosey squeezed Cole's hand. "Those are the people who need your help. I'll bet you weren't a bundle of fun when Garvey first met you."

Cole shook his head.

"How is your pain?" Rosey asked.

"I hurt," Cole said.

The Tlingit nurse unwrapped a packet and prepared a syringe and needle. "Let's give you something to help you sleep."

"Give me something to take away the monsters," Cole said.

"Only you can do that," she answered.

Cole slept hard, his first real sleep in many days. When he awoke, a small lamp glowed in the dark near his bed. Rosey was already up, working quietly around the room. When she heard him stir, she snapped on the lights and came over beside the bed. "Did you sleep well?" she asked.

Cole nodded.

"Let's clean your dressings this morning," she said. "The people in Ketchikan think we're witch doctors out here in the sticks."

Cole grimaced. The pain had returned with a vengeance. Rosey saw him wince and gave him another shot. "Things will hurt worse before they're better," she said. "Just warning you so you'll know what to expect." Then she added, "But they really will get better."

While Cole waited for the medication to dull the pain, Garvey sat upright on his cot and stretched the kinks out of his back. He ran a hand through his tousled hair. "How about if I get some breakfast?" he said.

Rosey nodded approval as she hung a fresh IV. Again she took Cole's temperature and pulse. Then she brought over a paper bag containing his clothes. "Here," she said, placing the bag beside the bed. "There wasn't much left of your clothes, but I had them washed up anyway to take with you."

Cole eyed the colorful at.óow blanket folded on top of the bag.

As Garvey returned with juice and warm oatmeal, Edwin appeared at the door and announced, "The plane is in the air. Should be landing in about thirty minutes." He turned to Rosey. "After Cole eats, let's get him down to the dock. I've got help coming."

By the time Cole finished eating, two boys from the village had arrived to help lift him. The boys, both Cole's age, eyed him curiously as they carried him on a stretcher out to a waiting van. Rosey rode beside Cole in the van, holding his IV bag. When they reached the marina, the boys again helped Garvey and Edwin carry the stretcher to the end of the dock.

Rosey hung Cole's IV from a dock post. "I'll be right back," she said. "I need your medical records from the van." The boys followed Rosey, leaving Edwin and Garvey alone with Cole.

Edwin looked out at the horizon glowing red with early dawn. "Tell me what happened out there," he said.

"I didn't think anybody cared about me anymore," Cole said, struggling to speak. "That's why I burned the shelter." Hesitantly, he explained how he had tried to escape the island and how he was mauled trying to kill the Spirit Bear. "I wanted to kill it because it wasn't scared of me," he admitted.

As Garvey and Edwin listened, he continued, telling next about the storm. When Cole had finished, Garvey said, "You may never have use of that arm again. Life is made up of consequences, and you've sure made some bad choices."

Cole nodded. "My arm isn't important."

Garvey gave Cole a puzzled look. "Why do you say that?"

"If I like the cake, maybe the ingredients are okay, too." Cole smiled weakly. "A famous parole officer told me that once."

Garvey raised an eyebrow. "A famous parole officer let you get mauled by a bear. Now you'll end up in a hospital. When you're released, you'll still have your parents to deal with and you'll still be facing a jail term. I doubt the Hearing Circle will consider returning you to the island after what's happened. You realize all that, don't you?"

Cole nodded. "I do, but it's okay. Whatever happens now, I'm done being mad."

Edwin shook his head. "A person is never done being mad. Anger is a memory never forgotten. You only tame it." He pointed out toward the islands. "Tell me more about this Spirit Bear."

"The bear was pure white," Cole said. "The last time it came, it stood right over me." He spoke in a whisper. "I reached up and touched it."

Edwin studied Cole. "Spirit Bears live hundreds of miles south of here off the coast of British Columbia, not here in these islands." He shook his head. "We've hunted here since I was young, and so have my parents and their parents. There are no Spirit Bears around here except maybe in your mind."

Cole started to argue, then remembered the handful of white hair he had pulled off the bear. "Want to bet," he said, reaching for his pants in the bag beside him. Suddenly he paused. His life had become filled with lies, and the more he lied the more he always tried to prove he was right. Never had he been strong enough to simply tell the truth.

Cole put down the bag. Today things would change. From now on he would speak the truth, even if it meant going to jail. He spoke softly. "I don't need to prove anything. I'm telling the truth."

Edwin narrowed his eyes at Cole. Then he turned and walked up the dock.

"Looks like I'm going to Ketchikan with you," Garvey said. "I need to go get my things. I'll be right back." As he turned to leave, he winked. "Don't go anywhere."

Cole watched Garvey leave. Finding himself alone, he looked out at the mirrored water. Maybe he had never really seen the Spirit Bear. He strained his neck to make sure nobody was watching, then reached into the paper bag and pulled out his jeans. Carefully he poked his hand into the front pocket and wrapped his fingers around something matted and fuzzy. He pulled his hand from the bag and opened his fist.

There in the palm of his hand was a wad of hair. Cole stared. The hair was white. All white. "It's true," he whispered. "I wasn't lying." Deliberately he raised his hand and tossed the hair into the water. Beginning today, he would tell the truth. His words would become his only proof.

As loud voices approached the dock and a plane droned overhead circling to land, Cole watched the white patch of hair. It floated on the water, and the breeze tugged it out away from the dock. The little clump bobbed about, drifting with the tide, then finally blinked from sight.

Smiling, Cole rested his head on the stretcher. Edwin had said that anger was a memory never forgotten. That might be true. But the Spirit Bear was also a memory that would never disappear from his mind or heart.

Part Two

RETURN
TO
SPIRIT
BEAR

CHAPTER 14

SIX MONTHS LATER

COLE HOBBLED SLOWLY but without help down the sidewalk leading away from the hospital. No longer did he have full use of his right arm. His many scars made him stiff, and limping helped ease the pain gnawing at his hip. Garvey walked patiently alongside. Cole's mother followed several long steps behind. Beside her walked the guard who had arrived to escort Cole back to the detention center. The guard watched with a close eye. He had wanted to handcuff Cole, but Garvey took him aside. A heated discussion followed. Finally, the guard nodded reluctantly and allowed Cole to walk freely during the transfer.

Cole's father had never once visited the hospital, nor had he chosen to be here today. Nobody mentioned him as the group crossed the parking lot toward a parked station wagon. His absence didn't surprise Cole. One month after Cole's return from the island, the police had arrested and formally charged his father with child abuse. He denied all the accusations, of course, and paid bail before the ink dried on the warrant.

He might have never been charged except for Garvey's words to Cole's mother. Standing beside Cole's bed in the hospital, he had said to her, "This is what has come from your silence. Keep quiet now, and you share the blame." The next day, she reluctantly agreed to press charges and testify.

During Cole's hospital stay, many people from the Circle had visited him, including his mother. Her visits had been the hardest. She spoke little except to wring her hands and ask, "How are you doing?" Each visit, she repeated, "I love you. You know that, don't you?"

Cole didn't know what to say at those times. Why now, all of a sudden, should he believe she cared? She visited every day, but that didn't prove anything. She still wasn't there at night. Nobody was there after dark when visiting hours ended, when Cole was left alone with his thoughts. That was when he relived the nightmare of the mauling and felt the ache of being alone, the fear, and yes, still, the anger. Edwin had been right. Anger was a memory never forgotten.

But late at night, Cole also remembered the baby sparrows. And he remembered touching the Spirit Bear. He remembered the white hair and the gentle eyes, black orbs that peered patiently at him through the dark. Remembering those eyes brought Cole a certain calm.

Cole hugged his lame right arm in close to his chest as he turned and glanced back at the hospital. It felt good to be leaving. It had been six months since the Spirit Bear sank its teeth into his hip and arm and raked his chest into hamburger. Even now, red puffy scars still crisscrossed Cole's body and served as painful reminders of the mauling.

Although his body had begun to heal, Cole knew that many more months of therapy lay ahead. "What happened to your body would have killed many people," the physical therapist had said. "You're lucky to be alive, and your body will continue to react to the trauma for a long time. You will never have full use of your right hand again. Some nerve damage and blood flow will repair itself, but you'll always have areas of weakness, numbness, and poor circulation. Damaged muscle and cartilage will stiffen your joints. Wounds will build scar tissue—that can cripple you if you let it. Fight back. Stretch, run, push, pull, anything to expand your range of motion. You are in a battle with your body now. Lose, and you end up crippled the rest of your life."

As they reached the guard's station wagon, Garvey turned to Cole. "The therapist told you only about your physical healing. That's the easy part." He pointed at Cole's head. "Healing up there is much harder. I don't know what the justice system will do with you now that you've burned your bridges. I'll stop by the detention center tomorrow and we'll talk."

"I'll stop by, too," Cole's mother said, her voice barely loud enough to be heard. Suddenly she reached out and hugged Cole, clinging to him. He heard her sob.

Cole felt embarrassed but did not push her away. Instead, he placed his hands on her shoulders until she released him. He swallowed a big lump that had grown in his throat. "I'll be okay, Mom," he said, crawling into the vehicle.

"Fasten your seatbelt," ordered the guard.

As Cole fumbled with the buckles, he nodded good-bye to Garvey and his mother. Now what, he thought to himself. As long as he had been in the hospital, he hadn't worried much about the future. Each day had been filled with surgeries and follow-up surgeries, physical therapy, daily visits from his mother and from Garvey, and a constant flow of visitors from the Circle wishing him well.

Cole peered out the side window of the station wagon as they drove across town. Would he end up going to jail now? And what would happen to his father? He couldn't picture his father in jail.

All too soon, the station wagon pulled to a stop in front of the detention center. Cole's pulse quickened as he eyed the familiar stark brick building. Obediently, he crawled out, letting the guard hold his elbow to escort him inside past the locked doors. He wore new clothes his mother had brought for him. All he owned now, including the at.óow blanket, fit in the small duffel bag he carried over his shoulder.

Cole found himself assigned to a different room than before. Not that it mattered. This one had the same plain walls, cement table, and bed. The only difference was the toilet. This one was dull green; the other had been tan.

When the guard closed the door, Cole walked over to the bed and hung the at.óow over the bed frame where each hour and minute it could remind him of the island. Then he sat down. He closed his eyes and drew in a deep breath. Sitting there, it was easy to remember the island, the storm, the cold, the lightning, the fallen tree, the dead sparrows, and the mauling. Now he would find out whether he could still remember the gentleness of the Spirit Bear.

When Garvey stopped by the next afternoon, he looked rushed. "Did you get settled?" he asked.

"How do you settle into a prison cell?"

Garvey smiled and pointed to his head. "It's all up here."

"Did you find out what's going to happen to me now?"

"Yes and no. As soon as it can be arranged, the Justice Circle will meet again with you. Because of what happened, they will probably relinquish authority over your case and send it back to the court system."

"Then what?"

"Then, I'm afraid, you go to trial and face sentencing."

"A jail term?"

Garvey nodded. "Most likely."

Cole looked down and picked at his thumbnail.

"How are you feeling about that?" asked Garvey.

"I'm wishing I hadn't blown my chance on the island."

Garvey nodded. "We all have things we wish we could do over again."

"Someday I'm going back to the island," Cole said.

Garvey glanced up curiously. "Any reason?"

"To see the Spirit Bear again."

"Ah, the great white bear," Garvey said.

"You don't believe I really saw one, do you?"

"You saw something, Champ," Garvey said with a frown. "Something chewed you up and spit you out."

"The bear didn't try to hurt me," Cole said.

"How do you know that?"

Cole hesitated. "When my dad uses a belt on me, I know he's trying to hurt me. I see it in his eyes. The bear was different. It was just trying to protect itself because I tried to kill it."

"Ever wonder why your dad beats you?"

Cole looked up, surprised. "I've never done anything to him."

"I didn't say you did."

"He just whips me 'cause he's mad."

Garvey smiled. "Remind you of anybody we know?" When Cole didn't answer, Garvey shrugged and walked toward the door. "I have to run, Champ," he said.

"You think I'm lying about the Spirit Bear, don't you!" Cole blurted.

Garvey paused in the doorway. "No, you're not lying. I think you *believe* you saw one," he said.

During the next week, Cole settled into the monotonous routine of the detention center. His father still didn't visit. Each day, however, Garvey stopped by, as did Cole's mother. His mother seemed a little different now, happier, and more sure of herself. She wore casual clothes to visit instead of dressing up.

"Maybe when this is all over, we can go start a new life somewhere," she said one day.

"It will never be over," Cole said.

"That's up to us," she said. "I've quit drinking."

Cole studied his mother. "Why?"

A faraway look crept into her eyes. "Nineteen years ago, when your father and I were newly married, we were just like any other young couple—in love and full of dreams. We dreamed of having you, raising you, and having an ideal family. We never meant for things to turn out this way."

"What happened?"

"Somewhere we took a wrong turn. Life got to be more than we could handle. Your father carried too much baggage from his past—baggage he never dealt with."

"What do you mean, 'baggage'?"

She smiled sadly. "Your father isn't a bad person, but when he was younger, he had parents who beat him for everything he did. That's all he ever knew. When I saw him start doing it to you, I kept telling myself things would get better. Drinking helped me ignore reality." She shook her head. "It took a divorce and you ending up in the hospital to wake me up. I realized I couldn't change your father, but I could change me. I'm sorry you've gone through all you have. Can you ever forgive me?"

"You weren't the one who hit me."

"No, but I didn't try to stop it. I wasn't there when you needed me."

"It's okay," Cole said.

"No, it's not okay, but maybe we can change things."

Cole studied her curiously. "This is the first time you've ever talked to me about this."

She touched his hand. "This is the first time you've been mauled by a bear." Then she gave Cole a big hug.

Cole clung to his mother even after she let go, then turned away to hide his misty eyes.

One week later, Garvey announced, "The Justice Circle meets tomorrow night. I'll stop by to ride over with you."

"Does Mom know?"

Garvey nodded. "And so does your dad. By the way, we have a little surprise for you tomorrow night."

"What's that?"

Garvey gave no answer as he left.

* * *

True to his word, Garvey arrived the following evening. Cole was surprised that the guard did not handcuff him as long as Garvey accompanied them.

They arrived at the public library a little after seven o'clock. Already the Circle had gathered. Cole recognized most of the faces as those from the old Circle, including his lawyer, Nathaniel Blackwood. Peter's lawyer was there, but Peter was missing, and so were Peter's parents. Also noticeably missing from the Circle was Cole's dad.

As before, the Circle began with the Keeper giving prayer while everybody stood and held hands. As they sat down, Cole noticed that Garvey kept glancing over his shoulder toward the door. Several times he checked his watch.

After introductions, the Keeper described briefly all that had happened and why they were gathered again. She told about Cole burning the supplies, trying to escape, and being mauled. Then she ended by telling how he had spent six months in the hospital.

That wasn't the whole story, Cole thought. She didn't know about the baby sparrows, the storm, trying to survive, how cold it had been, how alone he had felt, or that he had seen and touched a Spirit Bear.

"Cole's response to this opportunity was very disappointing," the Keeper concluded. "He broke his contract with the Circle, and he violated our trust. Is there anything more this Circle can reasonably do?"

One by one the Circle members held the feather and expressed their disappointment over what had happened. "My belief is that this situation should no longer be handled by the Circle," one member finally said. Most of the others nodded their agreement.

Again Cole noticed Garvey glancing toward the door. Suddenly the door opened, and everyone turned to look.

In walked Edwin.

The Tlingit elder seemed totally out of place here in Minneapolis. He still wore faded old blue jeans, but instead of his worn T-shirt, he wore a baggy sweater that covered up most of his potbelly. "I'm sorry for arriving late," he announced. "Here in the city you have something we don't have in our village: traffic."

The Circle members chuckled as Garvey asked permission to speak. The Keeper handed him the feather, and Garvey introduced everyone to the Tlingit elder.

"May I join your circle?" Edwin asked reverently.

The Keeper nodded. "Yes, please do," she said, bringing another chair into the circle and placing it immediately to her left.

As Edwin seated himself, he looked over at Cole and nodded. Cole smiled back. The Keeper motioned for the feather to continue around the Circle. "We were just getting ready to hear from Cole," she said. "Cole, would you please tell us why you have broken your contract with the Circle? Explain why we shouldn't transfer your case back to the court system for prosecution and sentencing."

CHAPTER 15

"I WAS MAD," Cole said, glancing nervously around the Circle. "When I went to the island, I wasn't thinking straight. I didn't realize you were all trying to help me. I thought sending me away was just your way of getting rid of me. I went there just to avoid jail."

Cole struggled with his words. "I . . . I know now I was wrong, and I know I can't go back to the island after what I did. That's okay." As he handed the feather to his mother, strong doubt showed in the eyes of the Circle members. He had lied to them so often, they were numb to his words now.

"I know Cole has changed some," his mother began, her voice surprisingly strong. "Since the attack, I've seen a difference in his attitude. For the first time, he's talked openly with me. I don't know what should happen to him now. I feel like I'm just trying to pick up the pieces myself." She dabbed at her eyes. "I just hope there are pieces left to pick up." She handed the feather on.

As each member spoke, nobody argued for Cole's release. Even Cole's lawyer spoke in terms of a reduced jail term for good behavior. Each Circle member expressed regret for what had happened. All of them thought it was time to return the case to the courts.

The only person to speak in Cole's defense was Garvey. "I don't know what-all happened on that island," he said. "But there has been a change in Cole; of that, I'm sure. Whatever we decide to do, I hope this change is allowed to continue."

When Peter's lawyer received the feather, she held it indifferently beside her as if it no longer held meaning. "This whole thing has to stop now," she said strongly. "No more! Too many people have suffered and paid a price on account of Cole Matthews. Maybe someday he'll find a way to be a productive member of society. For now, it's the welfare of society that must be considered.

"Two days on an island is hardly enough time to change someone. This Circle needs to know that Peter Driscal is not rehabilitating well, either physically or emotionally. He has slurred speech and diminished coordination. This is Cole's fault. It's not something Cole can fix, but he can face the consequences. Even now, he refuses to admit the complete truth. I understand he claims that a pure white bear attacked him. Does he really expect anybody to believe such a thing? I'm told no such bear exists in the area he was sent."

The lawyer spoke firmly. "Circle Justice has proven to be a waste of time. It's time for Cole to face real consequences." She handed the feather back to the Keeper.

The Keeper ran her fingers over the feather to straighten it, as if trying to fix the damage suffered by the Circle. When she finished, she turned to Edwin. "Do you have anything to share?"

Edwin nodded. "Can I ask Cole to help me with a demonstration?" When the Keeper nodded, Edwin stood and walked to the open end of the room. He motioned for Cole to follow him. Every eye followed their movements.

"Okay," the Tlingit elder began. "Let's pretend this line is life." He pointed out a seam in the linoleum flooring that crossed the room. He placed Cole on one side and stood himself on the other. "Cole and I are going to walk the length of this line as if going through life together. This line represents a bad path that I want Cole to move away from. I have two ways to get him away."

Edwin began leaning into Cole as they walked forward. Cole instinctively pushed back. They walked forward, pushing on each other harder and harder. Soon they were both struggling. When they reached the other end, Edwin had succeeded in pushing Cole only a couple of feet away from the line.

Breathing hard, Cole eyed Edwin with distrust.

"Okay, let's walk the other direction and try to do the same thing in a different way," Edwin said.

As Cole turned, suddenly Edwin rushed at him and shoved him hard with both hands. The push sent Cole sprawling to the floor, yards away from the line. Startled, Cole scrambled to get to his feet. Edwin offered a hand and helped him up. Cole fought the urge to hit or shove the elder. "You caught me off guard!" he said.

Edwin smiled slightly. "Yes, life does that a lot." He turned to the group. "People change two ways—with slow persistent pressure, or with a single and sudden traumatic experience. That's why people often change so much when they have a near-death experience. I believe something significant happened to Cole on the island. Six months ago, he would have come up off the floor swinging after a push like that."

Edwin paused, rubbing his rough hand over his stubbled chin. "And yes, maybe people don't change completely overnight, but I do believe they can change direction overnight. Facing in a new direction is the first step of any new journey."

"How can we be sure Cole has found a new direction?" the Keeper asked. "We've heard this claim before. He still claims he saw a white bear. Isn't that proof he is still lying to us?"

Edwin turned to Cole as they returned to the Circle. "Did you see a Spirit Bear?"

Cole thought a moment. He could lie, and they would all believe him. Or he could tell the truth, and they would all think he still lied.

"You don't need to think about the truth," said Edwin.

"I saw a Spirit Bear, and I touched it," Cole blurted out.

A thin smile pulled at Edwin's lips.

"That should be all the proof you need," exclaimed Peter's lawyer, although she no longer held the feather. "That should be the last time this Circle needs to sit here and listen to lies."

Edwin spoke. "Three weeks ago, the crew of a fishing boat returning to Drake claimed they had seen a white bear on an island near where Cole was banished. I might have questioned the report if one of the crew hadn't been Bernie."

"Who's Bernie?" asked the Keeper.

Edwin waved a hand. "Just a friend. But I've

known Bernie my whole life, and he's not a man to lie."

"I don't care if there's a black bear, a white bear, or a yellow one with green polka dots," said Peter's lawyer. "What matters is that Cole broke his contract with the Circle, and now it's time for him to pay. We give him chance after chance, and at the same time we tell him he has to face the consequences of his actions." The lawyer raised her voice almost to a shout. "No more chances!"

Cole breathed slowly. He felt strong enough now to face whatever happened. He was strong enough to not blame anybody else. He could admit that he was no longer in control, and he knew he could tell the truth. But could he control his anger? Even now it smoldered.

The Keeper spoke with a rigid voice. "We can't just build another cabin, buy more supplies, and start over as if nothing ever happened. Circle Justice isn't blind. It *is* about facing consequences."

"Why don't we just send him away to Disney World for a year?" said Peter's lawyer sarcastically.

"This time there would be no free ride," Edwin said. "If we sent him back to the island, Cole would build his own cabin, and pay for every penny of the supplies by selling things he owns and values. It would be much harder than before."

The Keeper spoke with resignation. "We have no way of knowing if Cole is over his anger."

Cole motioned for the feather. "I know I had a chance once and messed it up, so I don't expect to go back to the island." He shook his head. "Edwin told me once that anger was a memory never forgotten. He's right. When I was mauled, I didn't get over my anger. I still feel it, even now, sitting here in this chair. But I've also learned it takes a stronger person to ask for help and to tell the truth. I *am* telling the truth when I say I saw a Spirit Bear."

During the following weeks, Cole mentally prepared himself for the inevitable. He imagined attending a trial and hearing the verdict: guilty. He imagined being led in handcuffs from the courtroom and for the first time being locked into a real jail cell. The hardest thing was to imagine being locked up, day after day, week after week, month after month.

While Cole worked through his feelings, he exercised. For long hours each morning and evening, he lay on his small bed, swinging his arms and legs, arching his back, and stretching to keep his body from stiffening. Midday, he worked out on weights in the center group area. He found himself growing stronger, and he found that when he had angry thoughts, he could exercise himself into a sweaty frenzy until pain from his joints drove away his thoughts and left him spent. No amount of exercise, however, could bring strength back into Cole's right arm and hand. It was all he could do to lift a shirt.

Garvey explained to Cole after the second gathering that the Circle would continue meeting without him. He wouldn't say exactly why, but he did say that Edwin had remained in Minneapolis to attend the meetings.

During the next two weeks, Edwin stopped by to visit several times. He never said much, but he studied Cole the way a person looks at a chessboard planning the next move. When he spoke, he asked pointed questions without explaining himself. After each visit, he left without saying goodbye. All he ever mumbled was "Gotta go."

Nathaniel Blackwood stopped by unexpectedly one day to announce he would no longer be Cole's lawyer. Cole's father had refused to pay additional legal fees, and now a public defender would be assigned. Barely two days later, Garvey and Edwin stopped by together. They sat down on Cole's bed and stared at him.

"What are you staring at?" Cole asked.

"So you think you're changed, huh?" grunted Edwin.

"What difference does it make?" said Cole. He looked down at his feet. "I feel different."

"How so?" said Garvey.

"It's hard to explain," Cole said.

"You better try." Edwin's voice left no room for discussion.

Cole quit trying to think of answers with his head, and instead, let his feelings answer. "After I was mauled, when I thought I was going to die, I felt like just a plant or something, like I wasn't important. I didn't know why I even existed. That scared me. I know it doesn't make any sense, but I realized that I was dying and I had never really even lived. Nobody trusted me. I had never loved anybody, and nobody had ever really loved me."

Edwin and Garvey exchanged a glance. "So how did that change things?" Garvey asked.

"I don't know," Cole said, emotions welling up from deep inside. "I really don't know. I just know that my dad's not going to ever come back to say he's sorry. Even if he did, he couldn't change what he did. He couldn't take away the memories."

"So, you think this is all his fault, huh?" asked Edwin.

"No," said Cole, his voice trembling. "Mom said his parents beat him up, too. I don't know where the anger all started. All I know is I don't ever want to have a kid and beat him up." Cole wiped at his eyes.

"What makes you think you're better than your dad or his parents?" asked Garvey.

"I'm no better," Cole said. "I'm worse. Dad never ended up in jail."

"Not yet," Garvey said. "So if you are worse, what makes you think things can be different for you?"

Cole swallowed hard. "Maybe they can't be. Maybe I'll never change. All I know is that things happened on the island that I can't explain. I've never been so scared." When Edwin and Garvey didn't answer, Cole found himself irritated. "What's with all the questions?" he asked. "You two are wasting your time now."

"Are we?" Edwin asked.

Cole fought back the tears blurring his vision. "You two are the only ones who ever cared about me," he blurted. "It's not like I don't appreciate what you're doing. But I screwed everything up. I'm going to jail—can't you see that? Why don't you just leave me alone now and quit wasting your time?"

Garvey cleared his throat strongly and rubbed at his neck. "Edwin and I are probably the two biggest fools alive."

"Or maybe we remember our own pasts too

well," Edwin added.

"We still believe in you and think there's hope," Garvey said. "Because of that, we've stuck our necks out so far, we feel like two giraffes. Last night we convinced the Circle to release you to our custody."

"What do you mean, your custody?" Cole asked.

"You're going back to the island," Edwin said.

CHAPTER 16

SOUTHEAST ALASKA

COLE'S PULSE QUICKENED as the island drifted into view. It had been fall the last time he made this trip. Then he had been wearing handcuffs and had almost lost his life. Now spring air chilled his skin. Behind Cole sat Garvey and Edwin, joking with each other and gripping the gunwales to brace themselves. There had been a heavy chop ever since they left Drake an hour ago.

Cole looked back. It had been a month since Edwin first announced this return to the island and, true to his word, he had insisted that every penny of the second banishment be funded with the sale of Cole's belongings in Minneapolis. If Cole wasted this chance, nobody else would pay a penny.

It had irked Cole, watching his sports gear, including his dirt bike, snowmobile, bicycle, skis, and even his helmet, all sold through a newspaper ad like some junk at a cheap garage sale. He squirmed on the hard aluminum boat seat. The sale no longer bothered him. If he screwed things up now, he could lose much more than a snow-mobile.

As the skiff circled the point into the bay, Cole felt a rush of excitement. He scanned the thick-timbered slopes. Low, overcast skies made the forests as forbidding as he remembered them. Was the Spirit Bear still out there prowling like a ghost under the thick canopy of spruce trees? The thought of the big animal sent a shudder down Cole's spine. He kept eyeing the trees as the boat approached the shore.

"Jump out and keep the bow off the rocks," Edwin ordered.

Cole removed his shoes and flung them ashore, then obediently he vaulted over the side into hip-deep water. The icy cold grabbed at his breath and reminded him of his attempt to escape the island. That swim now seemed like a night-mare from another lifetime. He must have been crazy.

Wind blowing directly into the small pro-tected bay had churned up a heavy surf, and Cole fought to steady the heaving boat. It was hard not being able to grip strongly with his right hand. Garvey swung himself into the water on the opposite side and helped guide the skiff to shal-lower water. Then, with Cole struggling to hold the bow, Edwin passed ashore the heavy boxes of basic supplies they had brought to go with the building materials delivered earlier by a larger boat.

When the skiff floated empty, Edwin stepped into the water, and all three dragged the aluminum boat out of the surf, over the rocks, and well above high-tide mark. "Try to swim away in this water and it'll kill you," Edwin warned Cole.

"I won't be running away," Cole said, retrieving his shoes. Already his feet were numb from the water.

"We'll see, won't we?" Edwin said.

"So, what do we do first?" Cole asked, looking up toward tree line at the stack of building materials.

"*We* don't do anything," Garvey said. "Everything is up to you now. Edwin and I will stay a few days until you finish building the shelter. Any questions, fine, but you're carrying the ball now. You're going to prove your commitment. Get a fire going first, then set up the tent." The two men headed down the shoreline. Garvey called back, "Have supper ready in two hours."

Standing alone, Cole eyed the aluminum skiff sitting unguarded. If he wanted to escape, now would be the perfect time. He shook his head. This time he would stay. He began scouring the shoreline for firewood.

When the men returned two hours later, they found Cole still putting up the tent. "Why isn't supper ready?" Edwin asked.

Cole walked to an old plastic cooler and pulled out raw hot dogs. "It is . . . here." When he saw the two men scowl, he added, "Just be glad I didn't take the boat while you were gone."

"That would have been a real trick," Edwin said.

"What do you mean?"

Edwin reached in his jacket pocket and pulled out a spark plug. "Engines don't run without spark plugs."

"You didn't trust me," Cole said.

"That's right," said Edwin. "Garvey and I believe in your potential, but you haven't earned trust. Not trying to escape in the skiff is a good first step."

"What would you guys do if I refused to cook anything?" Cole asked with a wry smile, as he sharpened a sapling for a hot-dog stick.

Garvey crouched beside the fire and reached his palms toward the flames to warm up. "First, we'd get hungry. Then, we'd take you back to Minneapolis."

"What's the big deal if I fix a hot dog or not?" Cole asked. "It's not the end of the world."

"The whole world is a hot dog," Garvey said.

"What does that mean?"

"Go ahead, eat a hot dog and I'll show you."

Cole poked a raw hot dog onto the stick and held it over the fire. He hadn't realized how hungry he was, so he held the hot dog in the flames to cook faster. All the while, Edwin and Garvey stared patiently. When the hot dog was charred, Cole placed it on a bun. "Now what?" he asked.

"Eat it."

Cole squirted on a glob of ketchup, then devoured the hot dog. Edwin and Garvey kept watching. "There," Cole said, finishing. "I ate the hot dog. Now what?"

"How was it?" Garvey asked.

Cole shrugged. "Okay, I guess. Why?"

"That hot dog did exactly what you asked it to do. You asked it to feed you, and it fed you. No more, no less." Garvey held out his hand. "Pass me a hot dog."

Cole pulled another one from the cooler and handed it across the flames. Garvey took the hot dog carefully in his hands and examined it. "This is a fine hot dog," he said. "The finest I've seen all day." Carefully he slid it onto the stick. He started humming. Soon Edwin hummed along. For ten minutes they hummed the melody over and over.

All the while, Garvey patiently turned the hot dog over the coals, careful not to burn it. Finally, when the hot dog was a glistening, crispy brown, Garvey drew the stick back from the fire. "The song we hummed is a song of friendship," he explained.

"What are the words?" Cole asked.

"There are no words because each person makes up his own. That's how friendship is." As Garvey spoke, he rummaged through the cooler, pulling out salt and pepper, cheese, a plate, cups, and a tomato. He leaned a bun against a rock near the coals to let it toast lightly, then wrapped it around the hot dog.

"You going to eat that thing, or play with it all day?" Cole asked.

Garvey smiled and kept working. He cut the hot dog into three pieces on a plate and lightly shook on salt and pepper. Next he cut slices of cheese and tomato and put them on top. With a flair, he added a small circle of ketchup to each. Last, he poured three glasses of water. He handed one to Cole and one to Edwin. "This is a toast to friendship," he said, raising his glass.

After taking a drink, he handed Cole and Edwin each a piece of the hot dog he had prepared.

"That's your hot dog," said Cole.

"Yes, it is, and I choose to share it," said Garvey. He began eating, savoring each bite. "Eat slowly," he said, raising his cup again to toast. "Here's to the future." After each bite, he raised his cup for a different toast. "Here's to good health." "Here's to the sun and the rain." "Here's to the earth and the sky."

When everybody had finished eating, Garvey turned to Cole. "How was my hot dog different from yours?"

Cole shrugged. "You shared yours and acted like it was a big deal."

Garvey nodded. "Yes, it was a big deal. It was a party. It was a feast. It was a sharing and a celebration. All because that is what I made it. Yours was simply food, because that is all you chose for it to be. All of life is a hot dog. Make of it what you will. I suggest you make your time here on the island a celebration."

Cole scuffed at the dirt with his shoe. "What is there to celebrate?" he asked.

"Discover yourself," Edwin said. "Celebrate being alive!"

CHAPTER 17

BEFORE THEY WENT to sleep, Edwin showed Cole how to suspend the coolers of fresh food from high branches in case bears visited during the night. "Tomorrow night we'll dance," he said.

"What do you mean, dance?" Cole said.

"We'll build a fire and dance our feelings."

Edwin offered no more explanation, so Cole didn't ask. But long after Edwin and Garvey fell asleep, Cole lay awake in the tent listening to their deep regular breathing. The hard ground made his hip and arm ache. Outside the wind strained through the treetops, and deep in the trees, a branch broke. Memory of the Spirit Bear flashed into Cole's mind. Was the bear still out there, and was it angry? Or was it only curious?

Cole tried to fall asleep, but troubled thoughts hounded him. What was his mother doing right now? Was she thinking about him, too? And what about his father? Did he care about anything other than himself? Cole thought about his own troubles with the law and about all his troubles at school. He thought about Edwin, about Garvey, and about Peter. He truly did hope Peter would be okay.

As he tossed and turned, Cole found himself growing angry again. He tried to fight back the familiar rage with his memory of touching the Spirit Bear, but nothing seemed to ward off the bitterness and frustration that flooded his mind. Edwin had been right when he said that anger was never forgotten.

Cole thought about his past, and also about his future. Tomorrow he would begin building a shelter under the watchful eyes of Edwin and Garvey. Even with his bum arm, he'd probably do all the work while they sat around on their butts like they had today. And then what? What would happen after they left? Cole imagined the cold, the rain, carrying water, keeping a fire going, doing schoolwork, and long, long hours of being alone and bored. That wasn't much to celebrate.

Cole's angry thoughts repeated themselves like a stuck record until finally he slipped into a troubled sleep. Almost immediately a hand shook him awake. "Get up and come with me," grunted Edwin.

"What time is it?" Cole grumbled, his head

still numb with fatigue. "Where are we going?"

"Hurry!" Edwin ordered. "It's almost morning."

Cole clawed his way out of the sleeping bag and fumbled into his shirt and pants. The icy air had made his clothes stiff, and he shivered. He heard Garvey still snoring loudly as he crawled out into the brisk air. The faint glow of dawn showed over the trees and dimmed the stars as Cole started to pull on his tennis shoes. Edwin stopped him. "Put these on," he said, holding out a pair of knee-high rubber boots. "Tennis shoes aren't much good up here except around camp."

Cole was still pulling on the second rubber boot when Edwin headed out. "Let's go, before the sun comes up," Edwin said, setting off at a brisk pace. He had a small pack slung over his shoulder.

"What's the big deal?" asked Cole. His stiff joints ached as he hobbled to catch up.

"Morning shouldn't be wasted."

By the time they reached the stream, Edwin breathed heavily. His potbelly definitely wasn't from too much hiking. Without stopping, he waded into the water and used the edge of the stream as a pathway to avoid the heavy underbrush. He picked his footing deliberately along the slippery bottom, working his way upstream.

Cole followed, splashing along stiffly in the gathering daylight.

"You tossed and turned half the night," Edwin said.

"Yeah, I couldn't sleep."

"Any reason?"

Cole didn't answer right away. "Just thinking," he said. When Edwin didn't reply, he added, "My mind gets to thinking and won't quit. Like it's chewing on tough meat. It won't swallow a thought, and it won't spit it out. It just keeps chewing it over and over."

"And the thinking makes you mad, right?"

Cole nodded. "It's like my mind wants to be mad at something and it won't quit. Even now, I'm mad."

Edwin stopped beside a long rocky slope that rose several hundred feet to their right above the shallow valley. On their left the stream flattened out into a large, calm, crystal-clear pond. Upstream about a hundred yards, the stream gushed through a rock gorge, calming as it flowed into the still pool.

"We're going swimming," said Edwin, dropping his small pack to the ground. He slipped off his jacket and shirt.

"Are you nuts?" exclaimed Cole. "It's freezing!"

"Trust me," said Edwin.

"To do what? Kill ourselves?"

Edwin kept stripping. "Half of being trusted is to trust." He reached down and picked up a thin stick.

Cole eyed the stick warily as Edwin waded out into the clear pond. Hesitantly, he removed his clothes, glancing again at Edwin, who had already swum over and seated himself chest-deep on a rock ledge across the pond. Edwin's eyes were closed, and he held the small stick against his shoulder patiently. He breathed deliberately as if unaware of the cold.

Slowly, Cole waded in, gasping as the icy water rose around his chest. He held his breath as he pushed off the bottom and swam the last twenty feet. "Cripes, it's cold!" he exclaimed as he pulled himself up beside Edwin on the underwater rocks.

Edwin remained still, eyes closed.

Cole hugged his arms to his chest, but couldn't stop his teeth from chattering. The water nearly covered his shoulders. He felt stupid and vulnerable. What was he doing a million miles from nowhere, sitting in a freezing pond beside a bizarre Tlingit Indian with a stick? "What's the stick for?" he asked loudly.

Edwin opened his eyes as if coming out of a

sleep. Calmly, he held up the stick. "The right end of this stick is your happiness, the left end is your anger," Edwin said. He handed the stick to Cole. "Break off the left end and get rid of your anger."

Shivering, Cole took the stick in his fists and broke off one side.

Edwin shook his head. "You broke off the left end, but a left end still exists. Go ahead, break it off again."

Again, Cole broke the stick, and again Edwin shook his head. "Why did you leave the left end on the stick when I asked you to break it off?"

"That's stupid," Cole muttered. "The left end will always be there."

Edwin nodded. "People spend lifetimes breaking their stick to get rid of anger. But always anger remains, and they think they've failed."

"So if I can't ever get rid of my anger, why even try?" Cole asked.

Edwin reached and took the remaining piece of stick from Cole's hand. His fingers toyed with the wood as he looked up at the sunrise that had begun to glow warmly over the trees. Then he glanced over his shoulder at the dark storm clouds that hung menacingly on the opposite horizon. He waved the stick. "Is the sky sunny, or is it stormy?" he asked.

Cole looked both ways and shrugged.

"Depends on which way you look."

"If you looked only at the clouds, what would you say?"

"Stormy."

"Yes, and what would you say if you looked only at the sunrise?"

Cole's body had grown numb from the icy water, and his teeth chattered uncontrollably. "Sunny," he grunted impatiently.

Edwin waved the stick in a circle. "The sky, this stick, hot dogs, life, it's all the same. It's what you make of it. What you focus on becomes reality. Everybody carries anger inside. But also happiness. Those who focus on anger will always be angry. Those who focus on happiness will—"

"I don't have a choice," Cole interrupted, speaking almost desperately. "I can't help it. I don't go to bed and decide I'm going to stay awake tonight and be mad."

"Have you been angry since you entered this pool today?"

"No," said Cole. "'Cause I'm freezing my butt off."

Edwin smiled. "When I was banished to this island, I came to this pond to get rid of my anger. It gave—"

"You just said you can't get rid of anger," Cole argued.

"This pond gave me a choice. I could focus on the left end or the right end of the stick. I could focus on the sunrise or the dark clouds. It was my choice."

"So, unless I go somewhere and freeze every morning, I'll keep getting mad, huh?"

Edwin smiled but shook his head. "You only look at the left end of the stick and at the cloudy sky now because your experiences in life have made that a habit. Happiness, like anger, is also a habit. You learn to be happy one day at a time. But habits change hard. This pond will help you."

"What do I do in the winter?" Cole asked.

Edwin wrinkled his forehead. "Winter will be the hardest. Weather is bad, days short, the fire warm, and the stream too bitter to soak. You'll find yourself wanting to stay inside beside the fire where it's easy for your anger to fester like a Devil's Club thorn. You'll stare into the flames and remember bad times. In the winter, you'll need to find other ways of looking at the right end of the stick."

Cole felt himself growing dizzy from the cold and was about to protest when Edwin stood and headed to shore. Gladly, Cole followed. On shore, Edwin pulled out towels for each of them, and they dressed in silence. Cole noticed that much of the stiffness and pain had left his joints. Even his arm felt better. He turned to Edwin. "You know, the stuff you just told me makes more sense than all the weird things the counselors and psychologist have told me in school and at the detention center."

Edwin tapped Cole's shoulder with the broken stick. "That's because those people still think you can get rid of the left end of the stick."

CHAPTER 18

B Y THE TIME Cole and Edwin returned to camp, Garvey was up and had a fire burning. He sat on a stump of driftwood, sipping coffee and looking out over the bay. As they approached, he turned and pointed. "Look at the whales out there breaching."

Edwin nodded. "Those are the humpbacks after herring. They're following their instincts. Every spring they migrate up from calving grounds in Hawaii."

"I've never seen whales before," Cole said. "Except on TV."

"We'll dance the whale dance tonight," Edwin said.

"Is anybody hungry?" Cole said, lowering a cooler from the tree. He dug through the food for a box of cold cereal, retrieved a jug of water, then mixed some powdered milk and began to eat.

Edwin eyed Cole wolfing down the cereal.

"You might want something more than cold cereal to work on."

"That's all I usually eat for breakfast. If you guys want something different, fix it yourself."

Edwin and Garvey both helped themselves to bowls of the cereal. "Suit yourself. You're the one working, Champ," Garvey said.

"Aren't you helping at all?"

"We'll show you what to do," said Edwin. "But every ounce of work is going to be yours."

"But I can't nail with my bad arm."

"Then learn to use the other arm," Edwin said. "If you build the cabin well, you'll stay dry and comfortable. Build it poorly, and . . ." Edwin shrugged. "It'll be a long winter. I built the last shelter for you, and I built it well. I still feel hurt from what you did. If you burn this cabin, you hurt only yourself." Edwin handed Cole a pair of leather gloves. "Here, these will keep you from getting blisters."

"I might have a bum arm, but I'm not a wimp," Cole said, setting the gloves aside.

"Your choice," said Edwin, as he began showing Cole how to lay out the frame for the cabin.

By midmorning, Cole had connected four squared beams and set them on large rocks that served as a foundation. He nailed planks to the square frame. These he covered with plywood flooring, making a large, rectangular platform, roughly the size of his room at home. Each nail he drove took about ten swings using his left hand, but gradually his swings got better. As he worked, his stomach growled for food, but he wouldn't admit he was hungry, not in front of Edwin and Garvey. The two sat around the fire watching and offering suggestions. Everything had to be just right.

The sun was almost overhead when Cole finally had to stop for lunch. He was starved and felt half dead as he built up the fire and dug out spaghetti noodles and a can of sauce. He put them into a pan, which he balanced on a rock in the fire. "How come everything has to be so tight and exact on the cabin?" he asked. "I'm not living here my whole life."

"About ten thousand mice are hoping you build it loose," Garvey said.

Edwin motioned to the north. "When the first winter storm comes with fifty-mile-an-hour winds, you'll know why."

After their meal, Garvey showed Cole how to lay out wall panels on the ground. By now, big blisters had formed on Cole's hands, and, with a sheepish grin at Edwin, he pulled on the leather gloves. "Go ahead, say 'I told you so,'" he said.

"Pride has no place on this island," Edwin answered.

By late that evening, when Garvey suggested he stop work for the day, Cole's hunger again gnawed at his belly.

"How about some more cold cereal?" Garvey said.

"Real funny," Cole said, pulling out hamburger from the cooler. "Some of us have been working." The smile on Garvey's face irritated Cole as he pulled the gloves off his sore and blistered hands. He examined his work. All four wall panels lay ready to be lifted into place. There was space for a door and one small window facing out toward the bay.

It still bugged Cole that Edwin and Garvey wouldn't help with anything. He made up three hamburgers but deliberately put only one in the pan to cook. Edwin and Garvey watched him as he ate his burger. When Cole finished, he yawned. "I'm beat," he said. "There's the hamburger if you guys want some. I'm going to bed."

"You'll cook for everyone," Edwin said. "And then we all dance."

"Do you need your shoelaces tied, too?" Cole mumbled as he returned to the fire and began cooking again.

"Make us a feast," Garvey said. "Not just food."

Grudgingly, Cole cooked the last two hamburgers, covering them with mushrooms, onions, and cheese. He walked out away from camp while Edwin and Garvey ate.

After supper, Cole washed the dishes at the water's edge, gingerly rubbing gravel on the plates to clean them. The raw blisters on his hands stung like fire. It was dark when he returned to the fire and flopped down wearily on a stump.

Edwin had stoked the flames into a bright blaze. "Now we dance," he said. He stood and walked close to the fire. "All around us there are powers. There are animals like the whale, the bear, the wolf, and the eagle. There are powers like the sun and moon and seasons. And there are the powers inside of us like happiness and anger. We can feel all of these and dance to them. They all have much to teach us. Today, we saw the whale, so tonight we'll dance the whale dance. Each of us will tell what we learned from watching the whale."

Edwin curled his arms over his head imitating a whale's head and began to pace around the fire, dipping his head up and down as if breaking through the waves. He exaggerated his motions, ducking and diving, lost in his make-believe world. After ten minutes of moving around the fire, he slowed to a stop, then sat down.

Next, Garvey stood. In his own way, he began moving around the fire, jumping up and to the side to imitate a whale breaching. He made exaggerated expressions with his face. Around and around the fire he moved, finally slowing until he sat down and rested peacefully on a log near the flames. He looked up at Cole. "Your turn."

"I don't know how to dance," Cole said.

"It's not something you learn," Edwin said. "Feel it. Become a whale and learn what it has to teach you."

Self-conscious but also aware of the warning in Edwin's tone, Cole stood and began circling the fire. He bent at the waist and moved with jerky motions, trying to pretend he was gliding through water the way whales in the bay had. He kept looking over at Edwin and Garvey, imagining how stupid he must look circling the flames. He was glad nobody from school could see him.

Gradually he moved faster, trying to imagine a whale migrating thousands of miles, being led by instinct. Lowering and rising, Cole wandered off away from the fire, then pretended the fire was the goal of his long migration. On his way to the fire, he leaped back and forth, chasing schools of fish. Nearing the flames, he closed his eyes and leaped high into the air to breach. He landed on his hands and feet. For a few moments he stared into the flames, then sat down. He held his blistered hands tightly to his stomach.

After a time of silence, Edwin said, "The whale is graceful and gentle. Tonight, I learned those things."

Garvey nodded and said, "The whale is also smart and powerful. That is what I learned from my dance."

After several long minutes, Garvey said, "Cole, what did you learn from your dance?"

Cole had been thinking. "A whale migrates but it doesn't have a home." He picked up a small stick and traced in the dirt. "I feel like the whales," he said softly.

When nobody spoke for several minutes, Garvey stood. "This has been a good day," he said. "*Now* it's time to hit the sack." He turned and handed Cole a tube of ointment. "Use this on your blisters before going to sleep. And make sure you put a tarp over the firewood or it will be waterlogged by morning."

"Thanks," said Cole. He turned to Edwin. "What would a dance of anger be like?"

"That's the hardest dance of all, because you face your anger and release it."

"Will we do that dance some night?" Cole asked.

"You'll do that dance alone after Garvey and I leave. You'll do that dance only when you're ready."

Unlike the night before, Cole had no trouble falling asleep. He slept hard, waking only to shift positions on the rocky ground. With first light, Edwin again woke him by shaking his shoulder. "It's time to go to the water again," he whispered.

Cole rolled away from Edwin's hand. "Can't we skip just one day?" he groaned.

Edwin shook his shoulder again. "Not until your anger skips a day."

"Why doesn't Garvey join us?" Cole argued.

"Maybe he's not angry."

"Does that mean you're angry if you're going?"

"It means I'm going to *get* angry if you don't get your butt up."

Grumbling, Cole crawled stiffly from his warm sleeping bag. This morning his hip and arm hurt so badly he almost cried out. It felt as if cement had hardened in his joints. Cole looked out into the gathering light and the steady drizzle. The last time he saw this kind of steady drizzle, he had been fighting for his life. Now he was going swimming in a freezing pond. He couldn't believe this was real.

As Cole stepped from the tent, Edwin handed him a rain jacket. Without speaking, the two left camp and hiked to the stream in the shadowy dawn. From there, they once again entered the water and waded up the edge of the stream until they reached the pond. Edwin crawled under a large spruce tree and stripped off his clothes. "Place your clothes near the trunk to keep them dry," he said.

"They would stay dryer if I left them on and stayed out of the water," said Cole as he began undressing. Soon he and Edwin sat together on the rocky ledge. Edwin made no effort to speak.

"How long do we sit here?" Cole asked impatiently.

"Until your mind is clear and you have a choice between anger and happiness."

"I'm not mad today," said Cole. "My head's clear, and I feel like I have a choice right now."

"Then sit here until you're numb," Edwin said, his voice edgy. "Each time it gets easier. Someday you'll *want* to get up and come here."

"That'll be the day," Cole grumped, shivering. He felt his skin growing numb and his breath cooling. Finally, Edwin stood, as if some invisible timer had gone off in his head. Without rushing, he returned to shore.

Cole followed gladly. "I can't wait to get back and start a big bonfire," he said as they toweled off.

"This morning, you'll take time to meet your ancestors first," Edwin said in his matter-of-fact voice.

"Do what?"

Edwin didn't answer. He finished dressing, then walked toward the rocky slope beside the pond. As he angled along the bottom, he searched the ground. Suddenly he stooped over and picked up a round rock the size of a bowling ball. He ran his fingers fondly across the rough surface as if he had touched the rock before.

"What are you doing?" Cole asked.

"Touching my ancestors."

"You're too weird," Cole said.

Edwin handed the rock to Cole.

"What do I do with this?" asked Cole.

"Just follow me; I'll explain." Edwin started up the rocky slope. "Trust me."

"How far are we going?" Cole asked.

Edwin continued up the long slope.

Grumbling, Cole followed. As they walked, Edwin spoke. "Your life isn't an accident. Many generations of your ancestors struggled through life, learning lessons, making mistakes, just as you have. Each generation passed on to the next what they learned and all that they became."

After several hundred feet, Cole's right arm ached from carrying the heavy stone. He stopped and looked back. They were barely halfway up the slope.

"Pretend that rock is your ancestors," said Edwin. "Climbing this hill is your life. With each step, you carry your ancestors with you, in your mind, in your heart, and in your soul. If you listen, your ancestors reach out from the rock and teach you the lessons of their struggles. Hear your ancestors. Someday, you'll pass those lessons on to others."

Cole acknowledged Edwin's words with a weary grunt and struggled on without complaining. By the time they reached the top, he breathed heavily. He was about to drop the rock to the ground when Edwin reached out, took the heavy stone, and set it down carefully. "Treat your ancestors gently," he said.

Cole shrugged. "What are they, wimps?"

Edwin ignored Cole's comment. "I've carried that stone up this hill hundreds of times," he said.

"This very same rock?"

Edwin nodded.

"You mean you carry it back down again, too?"

Edwin smiled. "There's a better way. Once the rock is set down, it changes meaning. Now it becomes your anger. Go ahead, roll the rock down the hill. Roll away your anger."

Cole crouched and gave the rock a shove. He watched as it crashed back down the slope. "That should make the ancestors dizzy," he laughed.

"Imagine your anger rolling away," Edwin said patiently.

Cole was still chuckling about his dizzy ancestors. He couldn't believe he had carried a rock all the way up here just to shove it back down again.

"Each time you do this, you'll find more meaning," Edwin said. "And you'll learn respect."

"What do you mean, each time I do this? I'm not going to carry that stupid rock up this hill every day."

"Stay angry if you want—it's up to you. When I was here at your age, I found it was good to carry the rock every morning after my swim."

Cole turned to Edwin. "What makes you think you know everything that's good for me?"

Edwin drew in a long deep breath. "I don't. Nobody does. We all search for answers, the same as you."

"Then why do you keep telling *me* what to do?"

Edwin smiled. "That's the first intelligent question I've heard you ask all morning." He shrugged. "Maybe Garvey and I want redemption for our own mistakes in life. We were never able to help those we hurt."

"Well, it's my life," Cole said. "Not yours."

"We should have stayed in the water longer," said Edwin, heading down the hill toward camp.

CHAPTER 19

AFTER RETURNING TO camp from his swim, Cole smeared lotion on his sore and blistered hands. A movement caught his eye as he pulled on the leather gloves to start work. "Hey, look," he called, pointing across the bay. "Is that a coyote?"

Edwin and Garvey looked up at a ghostlike figure moving along the far shoreline. "It's a wolf," Edwin said. "A big one."

The solitary gray animal loped along the shore, stopping every dozen strides to look around and sniff among the rocks. When it reached the stream, it lowered its head to drink, then bounded across the shallow rapids and disappeared into the thick underbrush.

"Tonight we dance the wolf dance," Garvey announced.

Already Cole had begun framing the roof. He worked hard and deliberately without speaking. He wasn't mad; he just didn't feel like speaking to anyone today. Edwin and Garvey sat watching, occasionally offering bits of advice. By midafternoon, Cole had finished covering the roof rafters with plywood and began nailing plywood to the wall panels. Every cut had to be made with a handsaw. The rain made the wood slippery and the ground muddy.

In the late afternoon, Cole rolled black tar paper over the roof and tacked it down. Now the cabin was ready for galvanized roofing sheets. As he struggled to lift the awkward sheets onto the roof, wind caught at them. One sheet bent in half. Edwin and Garvey refused to help, even though Cole cast a few hard glances their way. Finally darkness fell across the bay, and Cole quit work.

"Next year, every trace of your existence here will be removed from the island," Edwin said. "Taking this structure back down will be your last chore before leaving."

"I'll just burn it," Cole grumped, as he headed toward the tent. "I've had practice with that."

"Where are you going?" asked Garvey.

"I'm hitting the sack."

"Not so fast, Champ. We're hungry, and you still haven't danced the wolf dance."

"I'm dog tired, and I'm not your slave. There's cold cereal over there if you want some." Cole crawled into the green canvas tent.

"Have a good sleep," called Garvey. "Tomorrow, we tear down the shelter and head back to Minneapolis."

Cole poked his head back out the tent flap. "What are you talking about?"

"You're finished here," said Garvey, his voice hard and absolute. "There's not enough room on this island for both you and your attitude."

Cole's thoughts raced. Garvey must be bluffing. But what if he wasn't? Nothing was worth that gamble. Cole stumbled from the tent. "Okay, okay, I'll fix you some supper."

"It's not about supper," said Garvey. "It's about the chip on your shoulder. You still think life is a free ride. You're still blaming the world for everything and looking for the easiest way to get by. It's only been two days, and already you've got your attitude back."

"I'm sorry," Cole stammered. "I didn't mean it."

"Don't apologize to us," Garvey said. "Apologize to yourself. It's your life you're betraying. Not ours."

Cole crossed from the tent to the fire and fed wood quickly onto the flames. Not a word was spoken as he prepared instant chicken casserole mix for Edwin and Garvey. He made extra effort to serve the food up nicely, but inside he didn't feel much like celebrating. He felt frustrated and desperate. Edwin and Garvey ate in silence.

"I said I was sorry," Cole said.

"You also said you had changed," answered Edwin.

"Please don't take me back." Cole's voice wavered. "I promise I'll try harder. I'll do anything you ask."

Edwin stood and faced Cole across the fire. "It's time to cut losses and send you home."

"I didn't mean what I said. I just—"

Edwin held up his hand. "Stop your mindless talking! Your words insult me! They're just noise in the air—they don't mean anything. Tomorrow morning, I want you to get up alone and soak. Then I want you to carry your ancestors and roll your anger away. When you return to camp, we'll see what you've learned." Edwin turned and headed for the tent. Garvey followed.

"Hey, aren't we going to dance the wolf dance?" Cole asked as he strung the coolers up in the tree away from the bears.

"We're going to bed," said Garvey. "You're the one who spotted the wolf. Do whatever you want—that's your usual program."

Cole watched as the men entered the tent, leaving him alone. The rain had let up, but a lonely breeze flapped the tent awning and chilled the night air. Cole was bone weary as he walked to the water to clean dishes. The tide was letting out, and he tripped, skinning his shin on the rocks.

Limping back to camp, he stood beside the fire, nursing his bruised leg. He felt as alone and frustrated as when he had been left mauled on the rocks. Edwin and Garvey didn't understand. They didn't know what it was like to be this alone. This afraid.

As Cole stared into the flames, he thought about the wolf. The wolf was alone, too, without anybody to care for it. Cole shook his head—that wasn't exactly true. Wolves often hunted in a pack. Together, they accomplished more than they could alone.

As Cole stared into the flames, he found himself crouching like a wolf. Slowly he inched forward around the flames, his head hung low as if prowling. Gradually he circled faster, pretending to run with the pack in pursuit of a wounded moose. He felt the power of the pack working together. The pack was powerful when they depended on each other. Any wolf that left the pack lost the protection of the other wolves and became weaker, no longer sharing the pack's food.

Almost reluctantly, Cole finished his dance. Trying not to wake the others, he entered the tent and prepared for bed. As he squirmed into his sleeping bag, a voice surprised him.

"What did you learn?" Garvey asked.

"That you need the help of others, like a wolf pack."

"Good night," whispered Garvey.

"Good night," said Cole.

Edwin coughed. "Have a good soak tomorrow."

Cole woke often during the night, afraid he might oversleep. He kept lifting the tent flap and peering out. When it seemed the night would last forever, the blackness finally softened into a dull gray. Cole could see the point of rocks at the opening of the bay. He dragged himself out of his bag. It was time to go to the pond.

The rain had let up, so he rolled his clothes into a bundle and crawled outside the tent to dress. Even without rain, the air had a brisk edge to it. Cole couldn't believe he was getting up this early to go sit in a freezing river. Maybe a jail cell wouldn't be so bad. As he headed out from camp, he wondered if Edwin and Garvey had been serious about returning him to Minneapolis. He kicked a small rock into the water.

Cole reached the stream and splashed along the bank toward the pond. Under his arm he carried a towel. He was so lost in his thoughts, a low hanging branch smacked him hard in the forehead. He bent over, grimacing, momentarily dazed. Then he continued.

When he reached the pond, Cole hesitated. It would be easy not to soak or carry the rock. All he needed to do was make up a good story before returning to camp. But something told Cole that Edwin and Garvey couldn't be lied to this morning. Immediately he stripped and waded into the icy water. The pool didn't seem quite so cold as the first morning they had come, but still it took his breath away as he crouched and lowered himself in. He held his breath and breaststroked over to the rocky bench.

Hugging his arms tightly to his chest, he sat shivering and looking around at the water, the trees, and the dawn sky. His whole body was peppered with goose bumps. He wondered how long he could stay in the pool. Edwin had sat calmly, as if sitting in a warm bathtub.

Cole tried closing his eyes. Maybe it would help to concentrate on something else. He drew air slowly past his lips and let it escape the way he had seen Edwin breathe. Over and over, he breathed, trying to clear his mind. Gradually, he quit hugging his chest and let his arms drift out and away from his body until they hung suspended in the water.

Cole found that if he sat completely still, his numb skin actually felt warm. He breathed deliberately, imagining himself as calm as the pond. Slowly his eyes opened, and he looked at the sky reflecting in the water. The floating clouds glowed red with the coming sunrise.

A flicker of movement in the reflection made Cole glance up, but then he realized the movement was a fish hovering near his knees. Holding his breath, Cole watched the silver fish. He wondered how the trout would taste for breakfast.

At the same instant he thought of eating the fish, it moved off and disappeared. Cole released his breath. Had he moved? Was that what scared the fish? Or had his thoughts exposed his presence? Surely the fish couldn't sense his thoughts.

When Cole breathed again, he noticed that his breaths had cooled as if he were sucking on a menthol cough drop. He also noticed that in the water, his joints didn't ache, nor did he feel pain in his blistered hands. His few thoughts seemed distant from his body. The cold water somehow suspended his whole existence.

When Cole finally left the pond, it was not because he had gotten too cold or impatient, but because he had finished his soak. He drifted forward in the water until he could breaststroke gently, barely rippling the calm surface.

On shore, Cole toweled dry. He felt he had discovered something, but wasn't sure what. All he had done was sit in cold water and try not to think, and yet that simple act had made him feel so calm.

After dressing, Cole walked to where Edwin's ancestor rock had stopped when it rolled down the slope the day before. He moved stiffly from being so cold, but his joints didn't ache as they had when he crawled from the tent early that morning. He paused before lifting the rock and slowly stretched his body, touching his toes, reaching for the sky, twisting at the waist, and leaning backward. All the while he kept breathing deeply. The deep breaths seemed to slow down his thoughts and make him calm. Cole wondered how Edwin had discovered this.

Cole kept stretching. Then he lifted the rock and started up the hill. He neither rushed nor dawdled. He moved deliberately, trying not to look ahead at how far he had left to go. Instead, he tried to imagine each step as a day in his life.

Whenever he stumbled, he imagined a day in his life when he had stumbled. There had been plenty of those days. But when he stopped to catch his breath, he looked back and saw how far he had come. He *had* come a long way since smashing Peter's head on the sidewalk. That seemed like another lifetime now. Cole wondered if the consequences of that moment would ever disappear.

Cole grimaced as he looked at the rock in his arms. He didn't want to spend his life in a jail cell. He hugged the rock tightly to his chest. What a fool he had been. Things *could* be different.

At the top of the hill, Cole lowered the rock gently to the ground and stood without pushing it. He couldn't stop wondering why he had been born and thinking about all the twisted events that had brought him to this moment. It seemed a bizarre dream to be standing alone on this rocky hillside in Alaska with a round stone at his feet, his mind filled with thoughts so totally different from anything he'd known running around on the streets back in Minneapolis. He felt like a new and a different person.

Slowly Cole let go of his ancestors and allowed the stone to become his anger. He knew that he had to quit blaming others, including his father, for his problems. As long as blame still existed, so would his anger. He had to let go, the same way he let go of this rock. With that thought, Cole sank to his knees and placed both hands against the rock. With a grunt, he shoved it down the slope.

As the rock tumbled faster and faster, Cole felt his body growing lighter, and when the rock smashed to a stop at the bottom, he felt as if he could fly. Now it was time to go back to camp and talk to Garvey and Edwin.

Cole started down, looking ahead toward the pond. A movement caught his attention, and he spotted a large white shape disappearing into the tall trees below.

CHAPTER 20

C OLE'S HEART POUNDED. Had he just seen the Spirit Bear? What else on the island could be that big and white? As he scrambled down the rocky slope, his thoughts raced. Did he dare tell Edwin and Garvey he had seen the Spirit Bear? They were already mad at him and would just think he was making up another story.

Back at camp, Edwin and Garvey sat beside a blazing fire, sipping cups of hot coffee. Neither spoke as Cole approached and pulled up a chunk of driftwood to sit on. After an awkward silence, Cole knew he had to say something. "I know that saying I'm sorry about my attitude isn't enough, but I want you to know that I am sorry." He paused. "When I was carrying the rock this morning, I realized that I won't ever get over my anger unless I quit blaming others for everything. That's why I got mad the last two days. I was still blaming you guys."

Edwin and Garvey exchanged glances. "So what made this morning any different?" Garvey asked.

Cole bit at his lip. "I just realized that I'm not a bad person. Nobody is," he said. "People are just scared and do bad things. Sometimes people hurt each other trying to figure things out." Cole gazed into the flames. "I hate what Dad does to me, but he must be just as scared as I am. He doesn't want to be mean; he just doesn't know any better."

"I'm glad you can see that," Edwin said. "But how do we know this isn't just another con job? Do you really expect us to believe you've changed?"

"It doesn't matter if you do," Cole said. "I'll be okay even if you take me back to Minneapolis." As he spoke, he noticed the plastic tarp had blown off his wood stack, so he walked over and tucked it back around the pile.

"If you're headed back to Minneapolis, why are you covering up the wood?" Edwin asked.

Cole allowed a smile. "Just in case you change your mind."

Edwin motioned toward the shelter. "Well, *just in case*, you better finish the cabin."

Cole wanted to tell them more about what he had learned that morning. Instead, he blurted,

"Thanks," then rushed over to continue work on the shelter.

"Doesn't matter, my foot," muttered Edwin.

Grinning, Cole pulled on his tennis shoes and gloves, and picked up his hammer. He worked hard all day. By dusk, he had finished the roof and framed in the single window. He also made a heavy door and mounted it with metal strap hinges. For the door handle, he screwed on a deer antler he found near the stream. He cut a hole through the door so the dead bolt could be locked from both sides. All that remained was to install the small barrel stove.

Glowing with satisfaction, Cole stood back to admire his new shelter. "So what do you think?" he asked.

Edwin and Garvey left their seats by the fire and walked around the small cabin, inspecting it.

"You'll need to keep a clean kitchen," Garvey said. "A determined grizzly doesn't need an open door to get in."

"And you'll need to do some caulking to tighten things up before winter," Garvey said.

"I know, but did I build a good cabin?" Cole asked eagerly.

Edwin and Garvey both smiled. "Not bad for someone who didn't care whether or not he stayed." Garvey winked.

"Shouldn't fall down," Edwin allowed. "Tomorrow, I'll show you how to run the stovepipe through the roof, and then we'll be leaving. You'll have the whole summer to build furniture."

Cole's body ached with weariness, and he stifled yawns as he prepared supper. Since this was the last meal with Edwin and Garvey, he fixed an extra good one. He boiled spaghetti, then fried onions and peppers to add in. While the sauce was simmering, he mixed some biscuits. A scrap of roofing tin propped up near the fire acted as a stove and baked the biscuits with its hot reflection.

"Where did you learn that trick?" Garvey asked.

Cole shrugged. "Just figured it might work." He brought over a leftover chunk of plywood and set it on stumps to make a low table. Trying to think what else he could do to make the meal special, Cole went to his duffel bag in the tent. He dug to the bottom and found the at.óow. He returned and spread the colorful blanket across the plywood like a tablecloth. Last, he rummaged through the supplies until he found a candle to place in the middle of the low table. "Grub's up!" he announced. "We're having a feast."

Throughout the meal, the cold breeze kept

blowing the candle out. Finally, Cole went to the cabin and brought back the glass mantel from his lantern and placed it over the candle. "This feast needs a candle," he announced.

When they finished the spaghetti and biscuits, he handed out Snickers bars from the supply boxes. "They aren't very fancy," he said. "But they're my favorite kind. If you eat them slow and close your eyes, you can pretend it's dessert from some fancy restaurant."

"Nothing wrong with this meal," said Garvey.

Edwin nodded. "It's good food. So, tell me, what dance should we dance tonight?"

"How about the Spirit Bear dance?" Cole said.

Edwin eyed him quizzically. "Did you see the Spirit Bear today?"

Cole hesitated before answering. "I saw something big and white disappear into the trees near the pond."

"Was it the Spirit Bear?"

Cole wanted so badly to tell the truth. He nodded.

"Are you scared of being here alone with the bear after what happened?"

Cole shook his head. "I'm not scared of the bear, but I am scared of being alone." He looked at Edwin. "How did you feel when you were here?"

Edwin looked deep into the flames, his far-away gaze conjuring up memories. "At first, I was so lonely it hurt. But with time, I felt peaceful inside."

With no further words, the three of them sat as if in a trance, staring into the flames until darkness fell. Finally Edwin looked up at the dark sky. "It's a great night for a Spirit Bear dance," he said to Cole. "You go first?"

"I need to think about it."

Edwin shook his head. "When you dance, it's your heart and soul speaking. You don't need to think. If you saw the Spirit Bear, you go first."

Hesitantly, Cole stood.

"In the village when we dance, we always beat a drum," Edwin said. "Do you want me to keep a rhythm?"

Cole shrugged. "Sure, whatever."

Edwin left the fire and returned holding two short chunks of driftwood. He sat down and began striking them together with a hollow knock. Again and again he hit the chunks of wood as if beating a drum. As the rhythm echoed down the shore and out across the water, Cole began moving. He let the story of his first visit to the island become his dance. Approaching the flames, then fading away into the dark, he appeared and disappeared. Each time he reappeared, he moved closer to the fire as if threatening to attack Edwin and Garvey. He hunched over, his movements ghostlike.

Then he flung himself to the ground beside the flames, clawing and kicking. In his mind, he relived the mauling. He grabbed at twigs and broke them as if they were bones. Grimacing on the ground, he heard Edwin beating the pieces of driftwood in a hypnotic rhythm. Cole raised his head and spit into the dark; then he pretended to lick up the spit. Last, he reached out as if touching the Spirit Bear. He froze in the touching position for a long moment, then stood and walked proudly off into the dark.

When Cole returned to the fire, he sat down.

Edwin handed the chunks of driftwood to Cole. "That was a good dance. Now you keep the rhythm."

Awkwardly at first, Cole knocked the pieces of driftwood together the way Edwin had, with a regular beat. It felt like the beating of his heart. Edwin stood and began to dance. He stalked proudly around the fire, sniffing at the air. Slowly, he came up behind Cole and Garvey. When they turned to look at him, he backed away. Again and again he repeated this movement until they no longer turned to look back. Then he came and knelt in front of them. That was how he ended his dance.

Cole kept striking the wood together for Garvey as he stood for his turn. Garvey started his dance lying on the ground as if he were asleep by the fire, then slowly awoke and sat up. He rubbed his stomach and licked his lips to show his hunger. Then he rose and moved around the flames, eating berries off imaginary bushes and catching fish from an imaginary stream. After several minutes, he stuck out his belly and scratched at it to show he was full.

Cole couldn't help but smile at his parole officer. This was the same man he had hated back in Minnesota. How could he have ever hated him?

Garvey spun around as if in surprise and gazed back at Edwin and Cole. He began prowling back and forth, back and forth, moving closer. He looked at Cole and placed a finger to his lips. Cole stopped drumming. In silence Garvey moved forward until he stopped less than a foot away. He crouched silently as if to touch his toes, then . . . "Boo!" he shouted, springing up, arms extended.

Edwin's stump tipped over, and he fell backward in surprise. Cole nearly choked catching his breath. Garvey laughed harder and harder until tears rolled down his cheeks. "Dances don't always have to be serious," he said. "Dances can be fun, too. Or they can be celebrations."

"You turkey!" Cole said, laughing himself. When he regained his composure, he grinned. "I understood both of your dances."

"And we understood yours, too," Garvey said.

Once more the three sat staring into the flames, each lost in thought. Finally Edwin stood. "Let's get some sleep. Tomorrow begins a new journey."

When Cole arose the next morning to go to the pond, so did Edwin and Garvey. "Mind if we go with you?" Garvey asked, as if he needed permission.

"That'd be great," said Cole.

Together the three headed out single file in the gathering dawn. Although this was only his fourth trip to the pond, Cole proudly led the way. When they arrived, he didn't hesitate. He stripped off his clothes and waded directly into the cold water. He found that by breathing deeply, he avoided gasping as the water rose around his chest.

He had already reached the rocks when Edwin and Garvey waded in. Edwin showed no reaction as he submerged, but Garvey caught his breath at the cold water. "Now I see why you two can't wait to get here each morning," he gasped.

"It gets easier each time," Cole said.

"Too bad I won't be around to find that out," Garvey joked.

The three sat in silence, looking upstream to where the water rushed through the narrow gorge. A cloud of light mist drifted over the river. Cole closed his eyes and ignored the men beside him. It wasn't the same having others here. Being alone was what made this place so special. Cole breathed deeply, once again feeling the icy numbness creep into his body. He opened his eyes once to see if Edwin and Garvey were ready to leave, then reminded himself that he would leave only when he felt it was time.

And finally it was time. With a final breath, Cole opened his eyes and slid off the shelf. Edwin and Garvey remained, eyes closed, but Cole felt no obligation to prove anything by waiting for them. When he reached the shore, he toweled off. He was half dressed by the time Edwin and Garvey left the water.

"So who's carrying the ancestor rock this morning?" Cole joked.

Edwin and Garvey eyed him without laughing.

"I was just joking," Cole said. "I'll carry it."

By the time they finished climbing the hill

and rolling away anger, a bright sun had broken through the clouds. They hiked back to camp laughing and joking as if they were old friends. Nobody ever would have guessed that this morning marked the beginning of Cole's yearlong banishment.

Edwin showed Cole how to install the stovepipe through the roof, and then he and Garvey prepared to leave. They took down their tent and loaded their belongings into the boat. Still they joked and kidded lightheartedly. When all was finally ready, the joking stopped. Garvey pulled out a small package and presented it to Cole.

Cole opened it to find a large hunting knife in a leather sheath. "Thanks," he said.

"That knife is like life," Garvey said. "It can destroy you or help you heal."

"How can a knife help me heal?" Cole asked.

"Use it to carve. If you discover what lies inside the wood, you'll discover what's inside of you. It helps you to heal."

"But you can never heal completely until you discover one thing," Edwin said thoughtfully.

"What's that?"

Edwin allowed a rare smile. "If I tell, you can't discover it."

As Edwin and Garvey crawled into the aluminum skiff, Cole called, "Don't forget to put the spark plug back in."

"It's been back in for two days," Edwin said, giving the starter rope a sharp pull. As the motor roared to life, Cole helped push the bow off the rocks. "I'll be out to check on you in a few days," Edwin shouted.

"I'll be okay," Cole shouted back, wishing he believed his own words. He watched the small boat until it disappeared from view. Standing alone on the shoreline, he couldn't help but remember how angry he had been the last time he watched the skiff leave. This time he felt only fear, and he admitted it. His palms were sweaty, and his throat tightened. If he screwed things up this time, there would be no next time.

CHAPTER 21

COLE DROVE HIMSELF hard after Edwin and
Garvey left, staying busy every waking
minute of each day. If he had to spend a
whole year on this island, he had no intention of
living like an animal. Each morning, he soaked in
the pond and carried the ancestor rock.
Afternoons, he worked improving camp. At night,
he slept like the dead.

By the time Edwin visited next, Cole had
built a table, a chair, and a bed frame for an old
foam mattress that was part of his supplies. He
made the furniture from driftwood, nails, and
scraps left over from the cabin. He also started
collecting armloads of firewood, cutting and splitting the wood with a small handsaw and hatchet,
and stacking it in a straight pile against the cabin.
Over the top, he placed strips of leftover plywood
and a tarp. For a bathroom, he dug a big hole up
among the trees. When the hole filled, he would
cover it with dirt and dig a new one. He didn't

look forward to using it in the winter.

Edwin said little during his first visit. He eyed the pile of firewood and the furniture with approval. "Garvey flew back to Minneapolis," he said as he crawled into his skiff to leave. "He was plenty worried about you."

"If you talk to him," Cole said, "tell him thanks again for the knife. I'll carve something special."

"What?"

Cole shrugged. "I don't know yet."

Edwin started the motor, backed away from the shore, and waved good-bye.

Cole watched the boat again until it blinked from sight. This time he didn't feel the desperate loneliness and fear of four days earlier. It would not be easy, but he knew now that he could survive. Instead of returning to the cabin, he headed around the shoreline to hike and think.

Wandering along the grassy flats above shoreline a mile from camp, he came upon a huge driftwood log. The weathered white log had been worn smooth and was straight as a telephone post. It looked to be well over twenty feet long and almost two feet in diameter. Cole tried to imagine what kind of storm could wash such a big log up a dozen feet above the high-tide mark. He remembered all too well one storm that could have done it.

As he examined the huge log, an idea came to him. Back in Drake there had been a whole field filled with totem poles. Most had carvings of animals the same as the totem designs on the at.óow. Cole didn't know what the figures meant, but he wondered if he could carve his own totem. Still he studied the log. There was something else this log would work for. The thought frightened him, and he pushed it out of his head. He would carve a totem, but how could he move the huge piece of wood?

Cole returned to camp and brought back two lengths of rope. He tied one to each end of the log. By tugging on one at a time, he rolled the log down over the rocks until it slid into the water. When he saw how high the log floated in the water, his mind again toyed with the idea that had scared him earlier. This log would make a great dugout canoe. It would make the perfect escape.

With the rope, Cole pulled the floating log slowly along the shoreline back to camp, using the last two hours of daylight to push, pull, and wrestle it up over the rocks until it rested near the fire. By the time he finished, it was totally dark.

Cole lit the lantern inside the cabin and made a jelly sandwich. He went to the doorway and stared out at the big log. Finally he slammed the door and crawled into bed.

For several hours he lay awake. Even after dozing off, his sleep was troubled. When dawn finally came, he felt groggy and rolled over for more sleep—it wouldn't hurt to skip the pond just one morning.

The sun was high above the horizon when he finally dragged himself from bed. Yawning lazily, he got out the cold cereal and sat down to eat, the whole while staring out at the log. If he carved a canoe, it wouldn't have to mean he planned to escape. Maybe he would use it for fishing, he told himself. But Cole knew that was a lie. He finished his dish of cold cereal then walked out to the log. He picked up the hatchet and began swinging hard, shaping a bow. By early afternoon, the end of the driftwood log had been roughly formed into a flat point. Cole felt angrier each time he rested. His only satisfaction came from swatting horseflies and mosquitoes. Never again would those little bloodsuckers feed off him like a carcass.

Overhead a pair of eagles worked the shoreline looking for fish. Suddenly one dove toward the water. It struck the surface with its talons and rose back into the sky, carrying a large struggling fish. Cole watched, fingering the hatchet in his hands. This was the first day he had felt angry since Edwin and Garvey left. This was also the first day he had skipped going to the pond. He spit at the wood shavings. He had just slept badly, he told himself.

Again Cole knew he was lying. He had slept poorly because he had considered making a canoe instead of a totem. Taking a deep breath, he lifted the hatchet and began striking the center of the log. Again and again he hacked, until a deep groove circled the log. With each blow, he felt his anger disappearing.

When the log could no longer be used as a canoe, Cole pulled out the knife Garvey had given him and began whittling and shaping the deep groove into an eagle's head. As he carved, he thought about the eagles he had seen and why they were such proud and powerful hunters. He continued carving until dark.

After eating supper and cleaning up, Cole went out to the fire pit and built a fire. He waited patiently until the flames burned high, then began to dance the eagle dance. Around and around the fire he circled, his arms spread like wings, banking left and right. Tonight he soared on the thermals and the air currents, seeing things that only an eagle could see.

After a long dance, Cole finally sat on a stump near the fire to catch his breath. His thoughts still moved high above the trees. He wished that somehow he could always stay part eagle in his mind. How could he remember to stay strong and proud, seeing everything in life differently from a distance? As Cole sat staring at the flames, it began to drizzle, and finally he got up and went inside the cabin. The dance had helped to ease the stiff pain in his hip and arm. When he fell asleep that night, he slept hard and dreamed of soaring high.

The next morning Cole awoke early and went for a soak. Afterward, as he carried the rock, he had to admit it felt good to return to the pond. He watched for the Spirit Bear, but saw nothing. Since returning to the island, he had caught only one fleeting glimpse.

During Edwin's next visit, as they dragged the skiff up on the rocks, Cole asked, "Why have I only seen the Spirit Bear once since coming back? I've seen plenty of tracks, but last time I was here, I saw it a bunch of times, especially after I got mauled."

Edwin lifted a heavy box of supplies and headed toward the cabin. "At first it was probably the bear's curiosity," he said. "Maybe after being mauled you were invisible."

"What do you mean invisible?"

Edwin didn't answer the question. "Have you

finished your schoolwork?" he asked.

Cole nodded and handed Edwin his completed lessons. "Any mail?"

Edwin folded the homework into his jacket pocket. "There's been mail, but we're not allowing you any contact with the outside world. I can tell you this: Garvey said your mom calls him almost every day to ask how you're doing."

Cole held back his emotions. "I think of her, too. How's Dad?"

Edwin shrugged. "After he was arrested, his lawyer got him released the same day. He never spent a single night in jail."

"Will I ever have to live with him again?" Cole asked.

"I can't answer that question," Edwin said.

"How is Peter?"

"Not well. Garvey says his bouts of depression keep getting worse."

"I wish I could help him somehow."

Edwin turned and studied Cole. "I think you're getting closer to understanding the secret of healing." Entering camp, Edwin spotted the totem Cole was carving and walked over to see it. First he examined the tapered butt of the log, then the half-carved eagle. His voice turned hard. "It looks like you tried to carve a canoe."

Staring down at the ground and speaking

almost in a whisper, Cole said, "I started making a canoe, but I knew that was wrong, so I cut this deep groove so I couldn't try again. When I started carving the eagle, I finally slept good." Cole ended by telling about his eagle dance and what he had learned. "Are you mad at me?" he asked.

"I'm proud that you carved a totem and were honest with me," Edwin said.

Cole paused. "You said I wouldn't heal all the way until I discovered one thing. Can't you just tell me what that is? I don't feel like I'm healing at all."

Edwin shook his head. "You'll discover what it is when you're ready to understand."

"Then tell me this," Cole said. "What are totems for?"

"They tell ancestry," Edwin explained. "And they tell stories."

"But how come they mostly have animals?"

"Animals are symbols. Tlingit tribes have two divisions—the Ravens and the Wolves. Closely related members form smaller clans. I'm from the Killer Whale clan."

"I'm not Indian," Cole said. "Does that mean I can't carve a totem?"

Edwin chuckled. "Indians don't own the trees or the right to carve. Carve anything you want.

Your totem is your story, your search, and your past. Everybody has their own. That's why you carve. That's why you dance the dances. That's why you live life—to discover and create your own story."

Cole listened quietly, then spoke. "I haven't created much of a story yet. I tried last week to dance the dance of anger, but I felt awkward, like I was pretending."

"You'll dance that dance when you're ready."

"When will that be?"

"You'll know."

CHAPTER 22

AFTER EDWIN LEFT, Cole spent the rest of the afternoon carving. At one point, a downpour forced him to roll the log close to the cabin. He stretched a tarp out from the cabin wall so he could keep working. By nightfall, he had finished the eagle. Already he had decided to carve a wolf next.

The next morning after visiting the pond, he washed his clothes in the stream. He built a fire in the cabin's barrel stove, then hung the clothes across the room on a makeshift clothesline. If he hung his clothes outside, they would never dry.

That afternoon, he tried to make himself invisible. He bathed extra well in the cold stream, then put on clean clothes. He even rubbed ashes and sweet cedar boughs over himself to mask any human smell. Then he hiked out to a point at the mouth of the bay where he could watch the shoreline both outside and inside the bay. He wedged himself down between two big rocks and sat totally still.

For two long hours he waited, but saw nothing. Frustrated, he got up and moved into the trees to try hiding beneath the thick undergrowth. The shore came gradually alive with seals, seagulls, and eagles, but no bears. Finally, chilled to the bone, he returned to camp.

Several more times before Edwin's next visit, Cole tried being invisible, but had no luck. One morning a beaver swam around him as he sat in the pond. At first, all he could see was a V-shaped ripple on the surface as the big animal swam closer and closer. Cole cleared his mind, breathed deeply, and sat completely still. The beaver swam even closer. Suddenly Cole reached out and tried to grab it. The beaver exploded in the water, slapping its tail with a loud whack before disappearing.

That was the only time the beaver ever came near. Cole regretted betraying the beaver's trust. He couldn't help but think how many thousands of times he had done the same thing to people. That night he danced the beaver dance. He realized that a beaver had persistence, patience and ingenuity. By using only its front teeth to chew down one tree at a time and dragging each one into the water, it eventually made a home that could dam a whole river.

The next day, Cole began carving a beaver's head. He tried to think about the lessons the beaver had to teach but he grew frustrated by how poorly he carved. His beaver head looked more like a deformed frog. Still he kept carving.

The air warmed with the passing of spring and the coming of summer. Some days not a cloud showed in the open blue sky, but most days were drizzly and wet. Cole had never seen a place with more rain.

Back in Minneapolis, Cole had thought that being alone on an island would give him plenty of time to just sit around. But just the opposite was true. Each day he kept busy cooking, carving, soaking in the pond, fishing, carrying the ancestor rock, washing clothes, doing schoolwork, and cutting firewood. Cole prided himself on how sharp he kept his knife and hatchet. Many nights he sat on his bed working them against a flat stone until they could shave paper.

Cole also continued to explore and look for the Spirit Bear, but still the bear did not show itself. Each night Cole tried without luck to find the feelings to dance the dance of anger. Weeks passed, but the large blank space he had reserved at the bottom of the totem for his anger carving remained empty.

During one of Edwin's visits, Cole expressed his frustration. "I've tried to be invisible," he said. "I hide and try not to smell like a human. I've even smeared cedar boughs and ashes all over my body, but I still haven't seen the Spirit Bear again."

"Maybe you still aren't invisible," Edwin said, climbing into his skiff to leave. "Have you danced the dance of anger yet?"

Cole shook his head.

Edwin pulled the starter rope and brought the engine to life. He motioned for Cole to push him out from shore.

Cole felt helpless as he watched the Tlingit elder disappear across the water. This time he had stayed barely long enough to unload supplies. Didn't he care? Was he mad? Cole returned to camp and spent the rest of the day carving. As he carved, two questions haunted him: What was the one thing that would help him heal? And how could he become invisible?

Many days Cole still fought hard to escape his familiar rage. It kept reappearing for no reason he could understand. At these times, he concentrated on funny and happy things. No matter how hard he tried, however, he still couldn't bring himself to dance the dance of anger. Long frustrated hours beside the fire brought angry movements, but the dance refused to come to him.

One day, after carrying his ancestor rock up the hill, Cole rolled his anger away, then sat down to think. Why had the Spirit Bear come to him when he lay wounded? Why had the beaver and fish come so close to him in the pond? He hadn't been invisible at those times. And why hadn't the bear showed itself again? Cole puzzled so hard his head hurt, but there seemed no connection. Nothing made sense. Finally he headed back to camp and worked the rest of the day in a sullen mood.

That night he went to bed as usual, but in the early morning hours, he awoke with a start and jolted upright in bed. He knew how to be invisible.

CHAPTER 23

T O BE INVISIBLE he had to clear his mind.
That was the secret. Cole stared up into the
darkness. In the cold pond, his mind
became almost trancelike. The fish and the beaver
had come close until he thought of hurting them.
The day he touched the Spirit Bear he had been
near death and had completely given up trying to
be in control. Being invisible had nothing to do
with being seen. Being invisible meant not being
sensed or felt.

This discovery excited Cole and set him to
thinking. If animals existed in a world of instincts
and senses beyond the conscious thoughts of the
mind, what happened to people in their frantic
worlds of noise and hectic rushing? How much of
the world did people miss because they were not
calm enough, empty enough, to experience it?
Cole's thoughts raced as he stared up at the black
ceiling of the small cabin. He couldn't wait until
morning.

When dawn finally arrived, he hiked to the opening of the bay instead of going to the pond. He made no special preparation except to wear a heavy sweater and rain slicker. The persistent drizzle and cold had become a daily part of his life here on the island. As he walked, he focused on the patterns around him.

The lapping waves came as regularly as deep breaths, the light drizzle roughed the water's surface, clouds hung low as fog, and thousands of smooth worn rocks lined the timeless shoreline like a ghost highway that disappeared into the mist. Cole felt a part of the patterns as he meandered along the shore.

When he reached the point, he picked a natural saddle between two rocks and sat down. He focused his gaze on a small white rock near the water's edge and breathed in deeply. To see the Spirit Bear, he needed to clear his mind and become invisible, not to the world but to himself.

He left his hood down to let his head and senses remain exposed to the air. The cool drizzle soaked his hair, and soon droplets of water dripped off his forehead onto his cheeks. When he closed his eyes, the droplets felt warm on his face. At first they felt like his own tears of anger and fear. Then he breathed more deeply, feeling the rhythm of the world around him, an endless rhythm where time disappeared. As the past, present, and future became one, the droplets on Cole's cheeks dripped to the ground, melting into the landscape to which they belonged.

When he opened his eyes once again, it was as if he were waking from a deep sleep. Far down the shoreline, where the rocks disappeared into the folding mist, a white object had appeared. At the place where things visible faded into not-being, there stood the Spirit Bear, as clear as if it were standing only feet away. The bear gazed patiently.

As Cole stared back with the same patience, all time, even the present, ceased to exist. He no longer thought of himself as Cole Matthews, a juvenile delinquent from Minneapolis, Minnesota. Instead he was part of the landscape, without a beginning or end. Rain dripped off the rocks that lined the shore the same way it dripped from his forehead and flowed down across his cheeks and lips. It blurred his vision, and he blinked.

The Spirit Bear disappeared.

Because Cole and the bear belonged to the same landscape now, Cole still felt the bear inside. He closed his eyes, still remembering.

When Cole next opened his eyes, he had no idea how much time had passed. He crawled stiffly to his feet and picked his way back along the shoreline toward camp.

That night Cole built a bigger than usual outdoor fire. He cooked his supper ceremoniously. With delicate pinches, he added spices to the boiling water. Then carefully he broke in spaghetti noodles. He heated sauce, stirring with deliberate strokes. When he ate, he savored every bite as if it were the last he would ever eat. When Cole finished eating, he washed dishes and carefully folded the at.óow, which he had used as a tablecloth.

Edwin had said that every day and every meal was to be savored, but tonight was extra special in Cole's mind. Today he had discovered how to be invisible, and now he was ready for the dance of anger. Carefully he stoked the fire once more and sat down to wait for both the flames and his feelings to come alive.

When the fire blazed high, Cole stood. Suddenly a frightening scream escaped his throat. As the sound melted away down the shoreline and into the trees, he began to dance. Spinning and weaving, he crossed the clearing to a solitary tree near the cabin. The tree was a tall cedar with only sparse scrub branches down low. Cole crouched before the solid trunk and doubled his fists menacingly. The tree defied him. That was why he had attacked the Spirit Bear. Its proud existence challenged him.

"Get out of my way," Cole ordered, swinging his fist as if to hit the tree. Again and again he warned the tree to move out of his way. When it remained, he lunged forward, swinging his fists within inches of the trunk. "Get out of my way!" he shouted. "I'm warning you!" When still the tree didn't move, Cole grabbed at the lower branches, all the while cursing and muttering angry threats.

The branches broke.

Cole continued his dance. He spun and lunged at imaginary enemies in the dark, yelling at the rocks and the sky and at the water, "Get away! Don't mess with me!"

Already his dance had lasted longer than any of his dances in the past, but Cole was far from done. The whole world was challenging him, and the dance grew more violent. Cursing wildly, he turned back to the flames and gave the burning chunks of wood a hard kick. Flames and hot ashes exploded into the dark. He kicked again and again, and soon the camp was a bed of glowing embers.

Cole stalked among the smoldering ashes. Grunting with effort and rage, he pretended to throw his spear, then fell to the ground and clutched his hip and arm. He grimaced as he relived the bear attack and the hatred he had once felt for the Spirit Bear. Twisting on the ground, he relived the pain, the cold, and the loneliness.

He continued his dance on the ground. As he writhed slowly on his back near the coals, his heart pounded a steady beat like a distant drum. He felt the storm that had killed the sparrows. He saw again the jagged white flash of lightning and heard again the crash of the huge tree that almost ended his life.

Still Cole continued. Standing, he walked to the shoreline and picked up a big rock. The rock became his ancestor rock as he walked in circles. Then, with an exaggerated motion, he heaved the rock into the water. When waves from the splash reached shore, he called into the darkness, "I'm sorry!" He screamed louder, "Please forgive me! I didn't mean to hurt Peter!"

The only answer Cole heard was the breeze pushing through the treetops.

Tears came to Cole's eyes and flowed down his cheeks. For several minutes, he let the tears flow, but he knew the dance must continue. Moving back to the fire, he spun among the dying embers on the ground with a graceful motion, gently kicking the larger coals back together. One by one he returned the scattered chunks to the fire pit, each piece becoming a part of his dance and a part of his healing.

The mound of embers and charred wood glowed brighter until a single solitary flame licked up, followed soon by another. Cole hugged his arms tightly to his chest and kept dancing. By the time the fire burned brightly again, sweat beaded his forehead and rolled down his cheeks with his tears. He was powerless to stop crying. His tears continued as if from some huge, bottomless lake.

Now Cole had danced half the night, but still a defiant flicker of anger remained inside him. He wanted to throw up that anger like bad food and be rid of it forever. He turned to face the tree he had threatened earlier. Again he lunged toward the tree, only this time he let his fists strike the trunk. With each lunge, he struck the tree harder, ignoring the pain.

Fists swollen and bleeding, Cole stopped suddenly. He caught his breath, feeling an overwhelming shame. In the middle of the night, he sank to his knees at the base of the tall cedar, his body shaking with sobs. "I'm sorry! I'm so sorry!" he whispered.

At that moment, words he had never been able to speak before welled up inside him. "I forgive you," he cried loudly. "I forgive you." Then, his energy totally spent, Cole collapsed to the ground. Now his dance was over.

The glowing embers cast faint shadows into the surrounding night, and under the trees, a large set of eyes reflected the light, staring patiently out of the darkness.

CHAPTER 24

THE NEXT MORNING Cole went to the totem to carve his anger dance. He stared at the blank space at the bottom of the pole. What figure or shape would express what he had learned during the dance? He knew one thing. Nobody ever woke up in the morning and chose to be angry. That meant that if he remained angry, something outside him controlled him.

Cole didn't like the idea of being under the control of anybody or anything. So what could he carve to show he was sorry and that he had learned to forgive? What could he carve to show the healing that had taken place and the understanding he felt? Cole left the space untouched and returned to the cabin.

"I danced the dance of anger," Cole announced during Edwin's next visit.

Edwin glanced at him. "What did you learn?"

"To forgive," Cole said. "Being angry is

giving someone else control of my feelings so they own me. Forgiving gives me control again."

"And what did you carve in the totem to show forgiveness?"

"Nothing yet," Cole murmured. "There's still something missing. It isn't enough to be sorry and forgive. Somehow I have to figure out a way to help Peter. Until then, I'll never be able to carve anything in the blank space. That's what I had to discover before I could heal, wasn't it?"

Edwin smiled slightly and nodded. "How to help Peter heal is something that will haunt you and stay in your thoughts like a sliver under your skin. The harm you did to him will fester and pain you all of your life unless you're able to make up for it."

"And what if I can't help Peter?" Cole asked, worried.

"Then you need to help someone else."

"Is that why you and Garvey have helped me so much?"

Edwin nodded, then turned and walked toward the boat. Cole could tell he was struggling to contain his emotions.

As the short North Country summer passed, Edwin's visits grew less frequent. When he did come to the island, he spoke little, as if something was bothering him. He stayed only long enough to unload supplies, pick up Cole's school assignments, and look at the totem. Each visit, the totem had a new carving, but Edwin always seemed to focus on the blank space at the bottom of the pole, although he made no comment.

By the end of summer Cole had carved a seal's head, a sparrow in a nest, and a raven. There were dozens of the huge black birds hanging out in the trees around camp, cawing for handouts at mealtime. Cole also carved a jagged bolt of lightning and a big raindrop after dancing a storm dance.

By September, the salmon began working their way upstream to spawn. Each day, during his soak, Cole watched them. He could see them leaping high out of the water, trying to make their way up through the gushing gorge of water above the pond. When the salmon run finished several weeks later, Cole danced their dance and carved their figure into his totem.

During late summer and early fall, Cole had spotted the Spirit Bear every few days as it wandered along the shore outside the bay or drank from the stream near the pond. But gradually, as winter gained a grip on the island, the sightings ended and the fresh tracks disappeared. Cole knew that the Spirit Bear had found a cave somewhere or dug out a hollow under a fallen tree to hibernate.

Cole stubbornly kept visiting the pond for his morning soak even though the water numbed him in minutes. Because of the bitter winds that winter brought, Cole spent more and more time holed up inside the warm cabin. Sometimes the winds blew so hard, the draft through the cabin blew out his lantern. He stuffed paper, cloth, moss, tinfoil, and anything else he could find into the cracks. Every two hours he got up during the night to stoke the fire. Nights when he failed to get up, he paid the price by having to start a new fire from scratch while he shivered in his underwear.

Carving on the totem became almost impossible. The icy cold stiffened Cole's joints and made his fingers numb and awkward. Several times he cut himself prying his knife against the slippery wood. He also quit trying to collect firewood. Now whole weeks passed without any letup of the rain. Everything became soggy, and Cole was glad he had cut and stacked a huge woodpile.

The last thing Cole gave up was carrying the ancestor rock and soaking in the pond. Walking over the frosty rocks along the streambed became too treacherous. Even when he hiked near the tree line, icy winds pierced his jacket and left him chilled.

Winter's daily routine settled into splitting firewood, carrying water from the stream, cooking, reading, and doing schoolwork. Any fishing now was strictly for food, not sport. Cole kept track of time with an old calendar he found in the supplies. Each night before going to bed, he took a pencil and marked off that day. When he turned the page to a new month, he treated himself to a candy bar. Edwin never brought many candy bars with the supplies.

Being confined allowed Cole more time for schoolwork, but also more time to think about being alone. Some nights he cried himself to sleep from loneliness. He couldn't help it. The silence became overpowering, and he longed to hear another human voice. He noticed his own voice getting hoarse and higher pitched from lack of use. If only Edwin would visit more often. The Tlingit elder's quiet presence was better than the endless hours alone.

During the long nights, Cole thought a lot about Garvey, about his mom, and about his dad. Had his father changed at all? And what about Peter? Cole still could not think of a way to help him. Edwin had said during his last visit that Peter was growing more bitter and depressed, hardly talking to anyone, even his parents.

Without the daily soaks and carving the totem, Cole found it harder to end each day with his mind clear and still. Sometimes anger crept back. It was as if it waited for him to blow out the lantern each night. Then Cole felt a growing resentment that he was being forced to endure this lonely existence. At these times, he imagined reaching up and touching the Spirit Bear. But he feared what would happen when he returned to Minneapolis and there was no ancestor rock, no soaking pond, and no totem. Would he still be able to find the Spirit Bear?

With his activities strictly limited by winter's harsh winds and bitter cold, Cole noticed his body falling into new natural rhythms. He found himself moving about at a deliberate pace, without rushing. He slept when he was tired and ate only when he was hungry.

Christmas came uneventfully. Cole hiked the shoreline a few days early and found a little scrubby pine tree barely three feet tall growing against the trunk of a larger tree. Figuring the big tree would eventually destroy the small deformed pine anyway, Cole chose it for his Christmas tree. He made tree ornaments out of aluminum foil.

On Christmas Eve, Cole sat alone in front of

his twisted little tree as the wind outside moaned through the treetops. Did anyone anywhere miss him at this moment? He went to bed early that night, not knowing the answer to that question.

The next time Edwin visited, Cole said to him, "Christmas was really lonely. I felt like the whole world had forgotten about me."

"Don't drown in self-pity," Edwin said. "You have more than most people. There's a whole box of your mom's letters waiting for you back in Drake. She knows you can't have mail, but she still writes every couple of days anyway."

"How is Peter doing?"

"He's grown more depressed. He no longer wants to get out of bed, and they have him on heavy medication."

After Edwin left, Cole couldn't stop thinking about Peter. He tried to ignore his thoughts by reading from a stack of books not part of his schoolwork. Getting lost in the stories helped him to forget, but only for a while. Some days he read all day and late into the night.

By the end of February, Cole had finished the last book in the stack and asked Edwin for more. Another few months and it would be time to leave the island. Still the space at the bottom of his totem remained empty. He had to figure out what to carve there before he left the island. At night, dreams of the empty space began taunting him.

One day near the end of March, Edwin stopped by for one of his visits. A cold drenching rain had been falling all day. When Edwin stepped from the skiff, Cole could tell that something was wrong. Edwin mumbled a halfhearted greeting as he pulled his boat safely up on the rocks. He silently picked up and carried a box of supplies toward the cabin.

Cole picked up the other box from the skiff and followed. Inside the cabin, he heated water while they dried off. Edwin sat beside the window and waited until he was almost finished sipping a cup of hot chocolate before he turned to Cole. "I got a call from Garvey yesterday," he said.

"How is Garvey?" Cole asked excitedly.

"He said that last week Peter tried to commit suicide."

"Suicide!" Cole caught his breath. "Why?"

"If someone is treated as if his life is worthless, he begins to believe it."

"But his life isn't worthless," Cole protested.

Edwin stood, and with one motion opened the door and flung the last of his hot chocolate outside.

"I never told him he was worthless," Cole argued.

"Smashing his head on a sidewalk is a funny way of telling Peter he's valuable."

"That was a mistake," Cole pleaded.

Edwin picked up his raincoat and headed into the pouring rain. "Hell of a mistake," he called back, pulling on his coat as he strode toward his boat.

Wearing only a T-shirt, Cole ran after Edwin. "I've said I'm sorry!" he shouted.

Edwin stopped in his tracks, and turned so suddenly, Cole nearly ran into him. "That doesn't help Peter." He turned and continued toward his boat.

"What more can I do?" Cole pleaded.

Edwin kept walking, ignoring the rain and cold. "I'm not sure anything can help now." When he crawled into the boat, he gave the starter rope a sharp pull and the engine roared to life.

"There is one way to help him," Cole blurted, but his voice was drowned out as Edwin revved the engine to steer the boat out away from the rocks. "You're not listening!" Cole screamed across the water. "I can help him!"

Edwin gunned the engine and angled out of the bay, refusing to look back.

As Cole watched the boat disappear into the

rain, he picked up a strand of kelp off the shore and gave it a hard fling. Maybe Edwin was right and nothing could help Peter. But maybe if Peter came to the island, he would see how much things could change. Peter was probably terrified; that was exactly why he needed this place. He could visit the pond. He could carry the ancestor rock and carve his own totem. He could dance, and maybe even see the Spirit Bear himself. Most important, Cole could prove to Peter this island held no monsters.

Long after Cole returned to the cabin and stoked the barrel stove, he kept thinking about Peter. How had Peter tried to commit suicide? And what if he had succeeded? Cole shuddered. If only Edwin hadn't left in such a hurry. Now it would probably be several more weeks before he came back with more supplies. By then it might be too late for Peter.

Cole knew that the idea of Peter coming to the island was nothing more than a desperate thought. No parents in their right minds would ever allow their son to come here alone, and certainly not to stay with Cole. Not after what had happened. Even with someone like Edwin or Garvey around, Peter himself would never agree to come.

Cole crawled into bed but tossed fitfully. He

remembered his own close brush with death and how terrified he'd been. It haunted him to think that Peter had tried to end his life on purpose. How scared must someone be to actually go searching for death?

Cole awoke well before sunrise. He dressed and went outside to go to the bathroom. The sky was unusually clear and filled with stars, and a warm breeze rustled the trees. Cole guessed that dawn was no more than an hour away. After returning inside, he stoked the fire, then pulled on his rubber boots and his rain slicker. It was months since he had last visited the pond. He knew the icy water would shock his skin like an electric fence, but this morning he needed desperately to calm his troubled thoughts. He had fallen asleep thinking of Peter, and he had awakened thinking of Peter.

Cole picked his way carefully in the dark. Life on the island had become a peaceful and almost boring routine that he understood well. Until yesterday, anyway. Now Cole trudged along in a confused daze.

Reaching the pond, he stripped in the darkness, then waded in without hesitation. The icy water stung his skin like fire. He tried to relax, but the cold quickly drove him to the shore. This water would kill him if he stayed in it long. There hadn't even been time to breathe deeply and clear his mind.

By the time Cole dressed and carried the ancestor rock, the sun had peeked above the trees. Then he heard an unexpected noise: the unmistakable buzz of Edwin's outboard engine floated over the trees. Cole took off at a dead run down the slope. What was Edwin doing back so soon? Cole scrambled and slipped along the edge of the stream toward camp. Dark shadows from the trees fell across his path and made the going treacherous. Several times he slipped on icy rocks and sprawled flat in the shallow water.

Cole arrived in camp breathing hard. He found Edwin inside the cabin, waiting calmly by the window. "What are you doing here?" Cole stammered, his teeth chattering. Water dripped from his wet clothes onto the bare plywood floor.

"What did you do, go swimming with your clothes on?" Edwin asked.

"I heard your engine, so I ran back from the pond. I slipped some. What are you doing here?"

"Get some dry clothes on," Edwin said.

While Cole changed, Edwin sat gazing out the window, his thoughts far beyond the bay and the island. Finally Cole sat down on the edge of the bed. "Why are you here?" he asked.

Edwin picked at the rough edge of the table

with his thick chipped thumbnail. "Peter tried again last night to commit suicide. His parents are desperate." Edwin placed both hands flat on the table. "Yesterday, when I left here, you said that you could help Peter. And you hollered after me that I wasn't listening. Well, now I'm listening. Tell me what you meant."

CHAPTER 25

COLE TOOK A deep breath. "I think Peter should come here to the island."

"That's not possible," Edwin said firmly. "And you know that."

"No, I don't know that."

"His parents would never allow him here alone with you."

"Then you come and stay, too," Cole countered. "Peter needs to soak in the pond and carry the ancestor rock. He needs to learn how to be invisible and to dance and to carve his totem. He needs to see the Spirit Bear."

Edwin shook his head. "I have fishing season starting. And besides, I'm not sure being around you is what Peter needs."

"I know he's afraid of me and what I did," Cole said. "He thinks I'm a monster that's coming back to get him. Maybe if he meets me again face-to-face, he'll see I've changed. And maybe he'll see that he can heal, too."

Edwin rubbed at his stubbled chin. "How much have you *really* changed?"

Cole felt no anger, but he was tired of trying to prove himself to Edwin. He was tired of trying to prove himself to the world. "There are two choices," he said. "Give Peter the same chance I've had here on the island, or give up and watch him commit suicide. Which would you pick?"

Edwin shook his head. "It's not that simple."

"It will be if you don't do something soon. I *have* changed, but Peter's parents don't know that. They'll listen to you. Maybe Garvey could come with him."

"What makes you think that Garvey has the time to come out here to this island to baby-sit you? The world doesn't revolve around Cole Matthews."

Tears blurred Cole's vision. "This isn't about me now," he insisted. "This is about Peter. I don't know what else to say—that's the best idea I have." His voice broke. "I screwed up, and I'm doing the very best I can out here on this island. But it won't ever be enough, will it? I can't ever change what I did to Peter! And I can't ever change how you think about me."

"You're right; you can't change what you did to Peter," said Edwin, his voice softer. "But you have changed." He studied Cole, whose cheeks glistened with tears. He laid a gentle hand on Cole's shoulder. "Whatever happens, you have changed here on the island. Both Garvey and I know that, and we're very proud of you."

Before leaving that day, Edwin asked one more question. "Would you be willing to stay here longer if it meant helping Peter?"

"I'd stay my whole life if that's what it took."

In the days that followed Edwin's surprise visit, Cole spent long periods standing beside the totem log, staring down at the blank space still at the bottom. His dance of anger had really been the dance of forgiveness and healing. But try as he might, he could think of no shape, form, or object that he could carve to show healing. Nor could he think of any other way to help Peter.

Days plodded by slowly. Cole wavered, one day hoping that Peter might come to the island, the next day frightened of the idea. All the while, in the back of his mind, he knew he was a fool for even considering such a thing. No person in his right mind would ever go to an island in Alaska to be alone with someone who had beaten him senseless.

Nearly two weeks passed before Edwin returned. Cole was sitting in the cabin reading a book when he heard the high-pitched whine of an outboard engine along with the deep growl of a second engine. He ran to the shoreline in time to see two boats round the point and enter the bay. Edwin's small skiff led the way, followed by a large green fishing trawler. Both boats plowed along, their wakes spreading out behind them like huge fans on the glassy water.

Cole could see Edwin alone in the skiff. On the deck of the fishing trawler, two people stood together near the back. Someone else sat alone near the bow. Cole squinted. The person sitting alone on the bow looked smaller than the rest. Cole's heart raced as the boat drew nearer. It was Peter Driscal.

With the boats still a hundred yards out from shore, Cole recognized Garvey's stocky bulldog figure at the helm inside the cabin. And he recognized Peter's parents. What were they doing on the boat?

Garvey guided the fishing trawler to a stop a stone's throw out from shore and dropped anchor. Edwin steered the aluminum skiff alongside. In minutes, everybody had crawled into the small boat to come ashore. Everyone but Edwin wore heavy jackets and tall rubber boots.

Waiting alone on the shoreline, Cole gave a hesitant wave. Only Garvey waved back. Peter sat near the back, his head down. He glanced up once fearfully, then returned to gazing down between his knees. His parents simply stared.

Cole caught the bow as the boat landed. He steadied the skiff so everyone could crawl ashore. Garvey and Edwin both said hello as they climbed onto the rocks. Garvey even gave Cole a friendly slap on the back. Peter's parents nodded stiffly. Peter remained in the boat, glaring fearfully at Cole.

"Hi, Peter. I'm glad you came," Cole said.

Still Peter refused to come ashore.

Garvey walked over and took the bow. "Give him some space," he whispered.

Cole retreated up the rocks, and finally Peter crawled stiffly ashore. Edwin helped Garvey pull the boat up on the rocks and tie the rope off to a large rock. Cole glanced nervously at the group. After being alone on this island for so long, he was uncomfortable around this many people, especially Peter.

Edwin motioned everyone up to the fire pit. Peter took awkward steps, as if struggling forward into a gusty wind. The rest walked in silence except for Garvey. "How have you been, Champ?" he asked.

"Good, I guess," Cole answered.

"Been soaking in the pond every morning?"

Cole nodded. "It's been too cold most of the winter. The last few weeks I've been soaking as long as I can stand it."

Edwin stopped beside the fire pit and invited everyone to pull up a rock or a piece of driftwood for a seat. He worked at starting a fire. Peter pulled his chunk of wood away from everyone else and sat alone, gazing along the shoreline and out across the bay. After the fire was blazing, Edwin sat down, too. "You're all a long way from Minneapolis," he said. "We're not going to pretend this is anything it isn't." Edwin turned to Cole. "I have fishing season coming, so Garvey will be staying here with you and Peter."

Cole turned to Garvey. "How did you get time off?"

"I had a bunch of vacation time built up, and I took a leave of absence. Coming here was something I needed as badly as you and Peter."

Cole looked at Peter's parents. "Are you guys staying, too?"

Mr. Driscal spoke forcefully, looking directly at Cole. "Bringing Peter here might be a huge mistake, but we had no other choice. This has been harder for us than you can ever imagine. We'll be staying until we're positive that he's safe. Nothing is going to hurt him again."

Cole swallowed a lump that came to his

throat. "I'll never hurt anyone again," he said. "That's a promise."

Edwin leveled his gaze at Cole. "A lot has happened in the last two weeks. Garvey and I have lived on the phone. The Circle agreed to gather again for many long hours of discussion. Mr. and Mrs. Driscal, as well as Peter, have been forced to make one of the most difficult decisions of their life." Edwin raised a finger at Cole. "And all because of one thoughtless moment on your part."

Cole nodded weakly.

Edwin stood. "Tonight Peter and his parents can sleep out on the trawler. Garvey and I will stay here in the cabin with you, Cole."

Peter continued staring out across the bay.

"Cole," Edwin said, "I want you to tell everyone about your time here on the island. If it takes all afternoon, I want you to show us everything you've been through. Everything, from the first minute you came ashore until now."

Peter's parents eyed Cole curiously, but Peter remained silent and apart, digging his toe into the mossy grass.

Cole pointed to the shoreline. "It all started when Edwin and Garvey first brought me here a year and a half ago. Edwin had already built a cabin for me." With an embarrassed smile, he added, "The cabin was a lot better than this one I built, but I burned it down. I was so mad, I couldn't think straight. I hated Edwin, and Garvey, and you guys. I hated the Circle, and this island, and everything on it."

Cole pressed his hands against his knees so that nobody would see his fingers shaking. He took a deep breath and told how after burning the cabin down, he had tried to escape by swimming. He pointed. "That's where the first cabin was, and that's where I dragged myself to after trying to swim away from the island. The tide pushed me back to shore. I slept there in the hot ashes."

Cole told about seeing the Spirit Bear. "Edwin had told me about them," he said, "but he said they lived much farther south of here off the British Columbia coastline. When I saw one down the shore staring at me, I tried to kill it."

"Why did you want to kill the bear?" asked Mrs. Driscal. "What had it done to you?"

Cole paused, licking at his dry lips. "It made me mad that the bear wasn't afraid of me. I wanted to destroy anything that defied me. Does that make sense?" When nobody answered, Cole motioned for everyone to follow him. "Come, I'll show you where I was attacked."

Everybody stood to follow except Peter.

"Come, dear." Mrs. Driscal gently coaxed Peter by pulling on his arm. Reluctantly he got up and followed her. Again he walked awkwardly, stumbling often.

Cole showed where he had tried to kill the bear and told how he had been mauled. As best as he could, he recounted every painful memory of the next two days. He told how the bear had licked up his spit and how he had finally touched the Spirit Bear. He even told how he ate the mouse.

"That's the tree the lightning knocked down," he said, pointing to what was now only a rotting log. He found himself blinking back tears as he told about the baby sparrows. "I deserved to die," he said. "They didn't. But that was the first time I was really scared that I *might* die. That was when I first started thinking about my life and cared about something besides myself. And that was when Edwin and Garvey found me."

Cole talked about his rehabilitation after being rescued, and about returning to the island. He showed the group his scars and his bad arm. "If you want, I'll show you the pond where I go to soak every morning." When Edwin nodded, Cole led the way, explaining how soaking cleared his mind. He also told about seeing the Spirit Bear again.

When they reached the pond, Peter's father asked, "Will we see the Spirit Bear today?"

Cole shook his head. "I don't think so. Not with this many of us here. Tomorrow morning, whoever wants to can join me for a soak in the pond. Sometimes the Spirit Bear comes and watches me soak." When nobody volunteered, he added with a smile, "This time of year, the water is really cold."

After showing them the pond and the ancestor rock, Cole headed back toward camp. The group hiked quietly, each person lost in thought. When they reached camp, Cole explained how he had built the cabin, then he returned to the fire pit. "This is where I dance all my dances," he said. Last of all, he showed the group his totem and explained the lessons learned with each carving. When he reached the blank spot at the bottom, he hesitated.

"What are you going to carve down there?" asked Garvey.

Cole shrugged. "I haven't decided yet." He didn't want to talk about the uncarved space.

Before Cole could change the subject, Edwin spoke up. "Why don't you tell us why you haven't decided yet."

Cole struggled to keep his voice steady as he told of the long night around the fire and his dance of anger. "My dad has beaten me my whole life," he explained. "But I know now he never meant to hurt me. He was beaten by his father, and that's all he knew." Cole swallowed a big lump that had formed in his throat. "I learned to forgive," he said. "Not just others, but also myself." He turned and caught Peter looking at him.

"When I beat you up," he said. "I never meant to hurt you. It was all I knew."

"You still didn't say why you haven't carved anything in that space on the totem," Edwin persisted.

Cole's voice quivered. "Because the dance of anger taught me I can't heal until I help Peter to heal. He's the one I hurt."

"Leave me alone," Peter blurted, turning away. "I don't want your help!"

CHAPTER 26

THAT EVENING COLE fixed his favorite meal for everyone. As he chopped hot dogs into the spaghetti sauce, he told the group how Garvey had taught him that life was a hot dog. "Tonight will be a feast because we make it a feast," he said. As he cooked, it began raining. Everybody retreated into the small cabin, sitting crowded on the bed, chairs, and stumps that Garvey carried in.

When Cole finished preparing supper, he spread the at.óow on the small table. He explained the colorful blanket's special meaning. "I only use this when a night is extra special," he said. "Now, let's eat!"

Everyone ate off paper plates held on their laps. Peter toyed with his fork.

"Honey, why aren't you eating?" asked Peter's mother.

Peter looked up and blurted, "I'm not sleeping in here with him."

"It's okay, son," said Mr. Driscal. "Garvey will be here. He'll make sure that Cole won't—"

"You don't have to sleep in this cabin with me if you don't want to," Cole interrupted.

"That's right," Edwin said. "I've brought along a tent. Cole can sleep outside until you change your mind."

Peter eyed Cole with distrust, still refusing to eat. Half an hour later, he returned to the trawler with his parents to sleep. His food sat untouched.

The next morning Cole hiked alone to the pond. He soaked as long as he could, his calmness shaken by how terrified Peter was of him. How could he have once wanted someone to feel that way? No matter how deeply he breathed, soaking failed to take away his troubled thoughts. When he returned to camp, he found that Edwin had already brought Peter and his parents in from the trawler. They stood on the shore saying good-bye to Garvey.

Cole overheard Peter arguing with his parents. "But Dad, I don't want to stay here alone with him!" he pleaded.

"I've already explained; you won't be alone. Garvey's here. You'll be okay—this is something you *must* do."

When Peter turned and saw Cole approaching, he turned away. Cole went on to the cabin.

Before leaving, Edwin visited Cole in the cabin. "Mr. and Mrs. Driscal decided to leave this morning," he said. "They had planned to stay longer, but realized they can't protect Peter from himself. After yesterday, I think they saw that you are no longer the problem."

"He's so scared of me," Cole said.

Edwin poured a last splash of coffee in his mug and took a sip. "Be as patient with Peter as we've been with you," he said. "Don't crowd him."

Peter's father appeared in the doorway. "Can I have a word with you alone?" he said to Cole.

Cole glanced at Edwin, then followed Mr. Driscal outside. They walked together up into the trees, where they were out of earshot of everyone else. Mr. Driscal turned and spoke in a warning voice. "You have changed some since we saw you back in Minneapolis—I'll allow you that much. But I also want to tell you, we haven't forgotten for a second what you did to our son. Not a day goes by that we don't think back to when you assaulted Peter. None of our lives will ever be the same again."

Cole lowered his head.

"I don't like the idea of Peter being here one bit," Mr. Driscal continued. "We would never have forced him to come up here like this if we thought there was any other choice. After his second suicide attempt, Garvey convinced us that Peter needs to face you or be haunted by his memories the rest of his life." Mr. Driscal poked a stiff finger at Cole's chest. "If you do *anything* to hurt our son now, God help me, you'll go to jail until you rot. Do you understand me?"

Cole nodded. "Mr. Driscal, this island can help Peter. I know you still don't trust me, but that's the truth."

"I've warned you," Mr. Driscal said as he turned and headed for the boat.

Cole returned to the cabin.

"What did Mr. Driscal have to say?" Edwin asked.

"He just wished me a good day," said Cole, avoiding Edwin's eyes.

"Yeah, I'll bet he did."

"He has a right to be mad at me," said Cole.

Edwin set his cup on the table and headed out the door. "Stay up here in the cabin until we're gone," he said. "I'm leaving the skiff with Garvey in case you have any problems."

Cole watched through the window as everyone crawled into the skiff. Peter remained sitting on the shore. As Garvey motored out to the trawler, Peter glanced fearfully over his shoulder as if he thought someone might attack him. Even after Garvey returned to shore, Peter remained sitting by the water, staring at the trawler motor from the bay.

Garvey returned to the cabin. Cole got up from his seat by the window and went to the cooler. There were only four candy bars left. He picked out a Snickers bar and started out the door.

"Where are you going?" asked Garvey.

"I have to try something," Cole said. He walked slowly down across the rocks toward Peter. When he was twenty feet away, the sound of his footsteps made Peter look up.

"Stay away from me!" Peter screamed, scrambling to get up.

Cole backed away. "Peter, I'm not going to hurt you." He held out the candy bar. "I just brought you this."

"Get away!" Peter screamed again.

Cole crouched and set the Snickers bar on a rock, then turned and retreated to the cabin. He sat down again by the window.

"Give him time," said Garvey.

During the next half hour, Peter glanced at the candy bar several times but didn't move toward it. Finally Cole pulled out his schoolwork and began working on his math. After a full hour, he rocked back in the chair and rubbed at his eyes. "How are my parents?" he asked.

Garvey set down a book he was reading and looked up. "Your mother is doing great and sends her love. Your father has filed a lawsuit to have the abuse charges against him dropped. He's also filed for your custody."

"You mean he wants to take me away from my mom?"

"I think it's a matter of pride. He thinks he can always get his way and doesn't want anyone or anything to win out over him."

Cole traced the eraser of his pencil across the table. "I used to be like that."

"I know you did."

"Do you think he'll win?" asked Cole.

Garvey shook his head. "Over my dead body."

Cole set down his pencil. "I haven't talked to you in a long time," he said. "Thanks for standing by me and for everything else you've done. How can I ever pay you back?"

Garvey pointed toward the shore. "Pay me back by not giving up on Peter."

Cole looked out the window and saw that Peter was still sitting on the shore, but the Snickers bar was gone. Cole smiled. "I won't give up on him."

When another two hours passed without Peter moving, Garvey went out to talk to him.

Even after coaxing, Peter refused to enter the cabin until Cole had left and set up a tent nearly a hundred yards away.

All afternoon Cole sat in the tent. After dark, Garvey brought out some hot supper. "How long do I stay out here?" Cole asked, shivering as he wolfed down the warm food.

"How long does somebody stay scared when they've been beaten senseless?" Garvey asked bluntly. "Good night."

Cole watched Garvey return to the warm cabin. Garvey and Peter were sleeping, warm and comfortable, in a cabin he had made with his own two hands. Here he was, sleeping in a leaky tent in the drizzle and wind. Instead of starting a fire in the pit, Cole crawled into his sleeping bag and went to sleep early.

When he rose the next morning, he forced himself to crawl from the warm sleeping bag and pull on his stiff cold clothes. Before heading to the pond, he knocked on the cabin door and called softly, "I'm going to the pond. Anybody going with me?"

"What time is it?" Garvey asked, his voice hoarse.

Cole realized he hadn't looked at a clock in nearly a year. "It's time to go soak in the pond. That's what time it is," he said.

"Give us five minutes," Garvey said.

"I don't want to go soak in any pond," Peter mumbled.

"We'll just go along and watch," Garvey said.

Cole saw a lantern flicker in the window, and he heard movement inside. Soon Garvey and Peter emerged from the cabin, both wearing their rubber boots and heavy jackets. Immediately Cole set out through the dark heavy mist, walking slowly so Peter could keep up. He heard the distinct shuffle of Peter's awkward footsteps behind him.

When they reached the pond, Cole realized that he had forgotten to bring a towel, but it didn't matter. He could use his undershirt. He stripped and entered the frigid water. Peter and Garvey sat down on the bank to watch. It was nearly the beginning of May, but still the icy water pierced Cole's skin like millions of tiny needles. He waded in, forcing steady breaths until he reached the rock ledge on the far side. Eyes closed, he heard Garvey's muffled voice speaking to Peter on the other side of the pond, but he couldn't make out what was said.

Cole soaked until his breaths felt chilled, then he waded back to shore. His body had numbed to the bone, but he didn't rush. During the last year, he had grown accustomed to the icy water. No longer did it take his breath away as it had when he first came here with Edwin. "Do you guys want to carry the ancestor rock with me?" he asked, as he wiped dry with his undershirt.

"I've explained the ancestor rock to Peter," Garvey said. "We'll hike along and watch you."

Cole picked up the large rock and started up the slope. He led the way, never pausing or looking back. By the time he reached the top, his bad arm ached but he still breathed normally. Peter and Garvey both breathed hard, and heavy sweat beaded on their foreheads.

"Now my ancestor rock becomes my anger," Cole explained, setting the big rock down. He turned to Peter. "You can push it down the hill if you want."

Peter shook his head.

"I'll do it then," Cole said, giving the rock a hard shove. As the rock tumbled down the hill, Cole closed his eyes. "When I hear that sound, I imagine my anger leaving," he explained. He waited until the crashing rock came to a stop at the bottom, remained motionless for a moment longer, then opened his eyes and started down the slope.

Nobody spoke as they worked their way back downstream.

"Do you need help with anything?" Garvey

asked as they arrived back in camp.

"I need to collect more firewood if I'm going to be staying outside much longer."

"Do you feel like helping us collect firewood?" Garvey asked Peter.

Peter turned and walked to the shore, and stared off at the horizon without answering.

"What's his problem?" Cole said.

"You," Garvey replied.

"But I hope he knows we're collecting this firewood because of him," Cole whispered.

Garvey answered quickly, "I hope you know that everybody's up here because of *you*."

Cole began collecting wood.

Day after day went by with no change in Peter. He refused to speak, doing whatever Garvey asked of him but no more. He hiked along each morning to the pond but never soaked. When he ate or walked, he moved zombielike, in slow motion. Cole quit trying to make conversation with him.

Nearly two full weeks after Peter's arrival, they all hiked up the hill one morning with Cole carrying the ancestor rock. When he set the rock down at the top, he paused a moment to rest. Without warning, Peter reached down and gave the rock a hard shove. He stood with his lips bunched, watching until the rock crashed to a stop at the bottom.

"That was a good push," Cole told him.

The rest of the day Peter remained withdrawn as usual, avoiding Cole.

Three days later, while Cole was cooking lunch in the fire pit, a rock struck the ground only feet away. Cole turned to find Peter beside the shore, pitching stones into the water as if nothing had happened. Cole looked at the stone that had almost hit him and realized his hands were clenched into fists.

He never told Garvey about the stone, but he kept a close eye on Peter. The next incident occurred with Garvey along two days later as they were hiking to the pond. It was early in the morning, and Cole had just jumped from one rock to another in the stream. All of a sudden Peter bumped him hard from behind and sent him sprawling into the water. Soaking wet, Cole picked himself up. He found Peter watching him with a smirk.

"Why did you do that?" Cole asked.

"I didn't mean to bump you," Peter said innocently.

Garvey said nothing as Cole continued to the pond.

"I'm skipping my soak this morning," Cole

said, "because I don't have any dry clothes to change into. But I'll still carry the ancestor rock." As he turned to pick up the rock, he discovered Peter stripping off his clothes. The thin boy ran stumbling into the shallow water, holding his arms above his head. He waded forward, gasping and grunting loudly.

Peter never made it across to the rocks. When the water reached his chest, he turned and waded back out. His teeth chattered as he dried himself with his undershirt.

That morning, after they returned to camp, Peter seemed more relaxed. He spoke to Cole without being spoken to first. "Don't you get frozen when you soak in the pond?" he asked.

Cole smiled. "The first time I soaked last year, I thought my head would crack open and my toes would fall off. But you get used to it."

"I don't want to get used to it," Peter muttered. He headed toward the cabin without looking back.

As the days passed, the air grew warmer but the rain came daily. Every morning Cole hung his sleeping bag up in the cabin to dry off. "I'm going to give Edwin a leaky tent for Christmas," he complained to Garvey.

Peter returned to being sullen, refusing to

talk. Garvey went about each day, joking with both boys as usual. He kept delivering warm meals to Cole in the tent. Nearly a month had passed since Peter arrived on the island. Twice Edwin had stopped by to drop off supplies and to check up on them. He never stayed for long.

One day a hard rain fell, and Cole stayed inside the tent. Hour after hour, the steady downpour soaked through the seams, soaking Cole's sleeping bag and clothes. Midafternoon, Garvey brought out food. He stared at Cole, huddled with his arms wrapped around his knees. "Dang, it's cold out here, Champ," he said. "I'm going back inside."

"Thanks," Cole muttered. For several more hours, he sat and shivered. Outside, the rain kept falling, and lightning brought angry thunder to the sky. As night fell, a small stream of water trickled across the center of the floor. Everything Cole touched was wet, soggy, and cold.

He prepared himself for a long night. Tonight he wouldn't sleep much. He hugged his arms to his chest and let his teeth chatter. He hadn't been this cold since he had nearly drowned trying to escape more than a year ago.

Suddenly he heard footsteps outside the tent.

"It's warmer in the cabin if you want," called Peter's hesitant voice.

CHAPTER 27

COLE NEEDED NO second invitation into the cabin. Fumbling with the zipper, he crawled from the tent and sprinted through the cold rain. When he opened the cabin door and let himself inside, Garvey greeted him with a wink. Peter was seated on the bed and eyed Cole with distrust.

"Thanks, Peter," Cole said. After drying off and putting on new clothes, he heated water for hot chocolate. "Anybody else want something hot?" he asked.

Garvey shook his head.

"How about you, Peter?" Cole offered.

Peter shrugged.

When the water came to a boil, Cole made up two cups of hot chocolate and handed one to Peter, who took it hesitantly. "Why haven't we seen the Spirit Bear yet?" Peter said.

Cole sat down at the table. "We will." He blew at his steaming drink.

"I don't think there really is a Spirit Bear," Peter challenged.

"I didn't think so either when I first came here," Cole said. "Even after I saw it, I thought I had just imagined it." He pulled up his sleeve to show the long scars from the mauling. "But this wasn't my imagination."

"That could have been from any bear," Peter asked.

Garvey stood and stretched. "I'm hitting the sack." He pointed over by the door. "Cole, you sleep there, and Peter, you sleep in the bed." He handed Cole a rolled-up piece of foam. "Here— it beats a hard floor. Use one of my blankets tonight. Tomorrow we'll dry out your sleeping bag."

"Thanks," said Cole.

Garvey stretched out his own foam pad and positioned himself between Cole and Peter. "Whoever stokes the fire during the night gets an extra pancake in the morning," he said.

"I'll do it," Cole said. He didn't mind if he had to stoke the fire for the next month. It felt so good just to be warm and dry again. As Garvey blew out the lantern, Cole pulled the blanket over himself and lay back on the foam mattress. This sure beat a leaky tent. He glanced over into the dark toward Peter. "Thanks for letting me sleep inside," he said.

"It doesn't mean we're friends," Peter grunted.

In the days that followed, whenever Garvey left the cabin or walked to the stream alone, Peter took the opportunity to get back at Cole in some way. Twice he walked in his muddy boots across Cole's sleeping bag. Every time he passed by the hooks where they hung jackets to dry, he knocked Cole's jacket to the floor. At night, when he went out to go to the bathroom, he left the door standing wide open. Returning, he did the same. Cole slept the closest to the icy air and had to get up to close the door to keep from freezing.

The final straw came when Cole returned from a walk alone around the bay. He found the bear carving on his totem destroyed. Someone had taken the hatchet and hacked the carving completely away. A familiar rage burned inside Cole. He confronted Peter in the cabin. "Why did you wreck my bear carving?" He tried to keep his voice calm.

Peter shrugged. "You never really saw a Spirit Bear. Besides, what are you going to do to me? Beat me up again?"

"No, I'm not going to beat you up. But can't you leave me alone?"

"I suppose you've never done anything to me," Peter said bluntly.

Garvey listened quietly.

Cole had a sudden idea. "I know where there's another big log around the point that would make a good totem. If you want, we can drag it here for you to make your own totem."

"Why would I want to do that?"

"When you carve, it gives you time to think."

"I don't need to think—I need you out of my face. And besides, what would I carve?" Peter asked.

"Anything you want. If you see a whale, carve a whale. If you see a Spirit Bear, you can carve a bear. I've learned from every animal I've carved."

"There is no Spirit Bear," Peter challenged again. "It was just a regular black bear that hurt you. Probably an ugly one!"

Cole ignored the comment. "I'll help you drag in a carving log if you want."

Peter shrugged indifferently, but after lunch he followed Cole and Garvey down the shore to see the log. Cole carried a rope. With the three of them working, they floated the log back along the shoreline. By dark, they had maneuvered it up beside the cabin next to Cole's totem.

"So what should I carve first?" asked Peter.

"Whatever you want. What was the last

animal you saw?" asked Cole.

"I saw a mouse in the cabin this morning."

Cole smiled. "Then tonight we'll dance the mouse dance, and tomorrow you can carve a mouse."

"I'm not going to dance a dumb 'mouse dance,'" Peter said, his voice thick with sarcasm.

"Every animal has something to teach us," Cole said, When Peter didn't answer, Cole motioned toward the trees. "Let's collect firewood for the dance."

"*You* collect wood," Peter said, heading for the cabin. "It was your idea."

"I'll help you," Garvey said.

Cole nodded. "I'll start the fire now so we have good coals for cooking supper."

Peter disappeared inside the cabin, refusing to come out until supper was ready. Then he sat out away from the fire as he sipped soup and ate one of the baked potatoes that Cole had wrapped in aluminum foil and cooked in the embers.

After eating, Cole added more wood to the fire. He waited until flames licked high into the night air, then stood and approached the fire. "I'll dance first," he announced. Slowly he moved around the fire, pretending to sniff about like a mouse. Suddenly he scampered away from the fire as if frightened, then came back again, sniffing.

Finally, he pretended to eat a full meal. When he finished, he sat down. "My mouse dance taught me that a mouse is persistent and bold," he said. "Mice are survivors that make the best of wherever they are or whatever they have."

Garvey nodded. "That's a good lesson. Now it's my turn." He stood and moved around the fire. Garvey's dance seemed to mesmerize Peter, who watched closely, following every movement. After Garvey finally sat down and finished explaining that mice are often not noticed and see things others don't, Peter stood and began dancing. His moves were jerky and unsure, and he kept glancing self-consciously over his shoulder, but he continued to move. When he finished, he remained standing beside the fire without speaking.

"So what did you learn from your dance?" asked Garvey.

"I learned that I look like a stupid dork!" Peter said sharply. He turned and ran into the cabin.

Cole and Garvey remained by the fire. "He's never going to forgive me," Cole said.

Garvey shrugged. "Think how much your arm and hip still hurt. Wounds of the spirit heal even slower."

Cole thought about Garvey's words long after they went to bed. The next morning, he went out and began carving a mouse into his log instead of going to the pond. He didn't have the heart to carve another bear where Peter had destroyed the first one. The bear carving had taken nearly a week to finish.

Reluctantly, Peter came out and began carving at his own log. By late afternoon, both boys had carved mice into their logs. Cole couldn't believe how real Peter's carving looked. "That's unbelievable," he said. "Where did you learn to carve?"

"I think my mouse looks better than yours," said Peter.

"It does," said Cole. "But carving a totem isn't competition. Saying your carving is better is like saying your feelings are better."

Peter smirked. "Mine are." He turned to Cole. "Did you really see a Spirit Bear?"

Cole nodded and told how he had pulled a handful of white hair from the bear that mauled him and then thrown it away. "The only reason I always had to prove things was because I knew I was a liar," he said. "I threw the white hair away because I decided I was tired of lying."

Peter studied Cole as they went to the cabin for lunch. He sat quietly through the whole meal. After lunch he returned to his log to keep carving. "I want to be by myself," he told Cole.

Cole and Garvey looked at each other but

agreed to take a long hike outside the bay to look for whales. It was nearly dark by the time they returned. Hiking back around the bay in the gathering dusk, Cole could see Peter still carving, but not on his own log.

"That jerk!" Cole said. "He's messing with my totem again. Hey!" he screamed, breaking into a run. "What are you doing?"

Peter stepped back from the log as Cole came running up.

Cole stared down, dumbfounded. In the same spot where the bear carving had been destroyed, Peter had almost completed another bear. The new carving was so real, the bear looked as if it were stepping out of the log. "That's incredible," Cole exclaimed.

"Hope you didn't mind," Peter said.

"Could you teach me how to carve like that?" Cole asked.

Peter shrugged. "Depends on if you want to learn." He turned away and headed into the cabin.

CHAPTER 28

A S SUMMER CAME to the North Country,
group visits to the pond had become a
daily event, until the day Peter announced,
"This morning, just Cole and I should go."

Garvey had already pulled on his pants. "Are
you sure?" he asked.

Peter nodded.

Garvey turned to Cole. "What do you think?"

Cole eyed Peter and shrugged. "Doesn't matter
to me."

Again Garvey asked, "Are you guys sure
you're ready for this?"

"Yes," Peter said, his voice firm.

Cole nodded, but found himself a little scared.

"Okay, have a good soak," Garvey said.

Cole packed their towels in his backpack. He
paused, then slipped in the at.óow. He and Peter
let themselves out the door into the breaking
dawn and worked their way along the shore.
Neither of them spoke as they reached the river

and started wading upstream toward the pond. Peter stumbled along angrily, his fists clenched. An awkward and thick silence hung between them.

When they finally reached the pond, Cole couldn't stand the silence anymore. "I'm glad we came alone," he said. "It's time we were friends." He held out his hand to Peter, but Peter knocked his hand away.

"I'll never be friends with you."

"Look, Peter, I didn't mean to hurt you."

Peter shoved Cole, knocking him off balance. "You beat me up and smashed my head on the sidewalk until I was bleeding. They had to pull you off me. What do you mean, you didn't mean to hurt me?" His eyes were wild.

Cole had regained his balance. "What I mean is, I didn't mean to get so angry. I didn't decide all of a sudden to get mad and hurt you."

"And so now everything is supposed to be all right?" Peter shoved Cole again with both hands.

"No, it's just that—"

"Everything will be better when my headaches go away, when I sleep at night, and my bad dreams quit." Peter's eyes welled up with tears. "I can't walk anymore without stumbling. Sometimes I can't think straight, and my words don't come out right." He shook a fist in Cole's face. "You don't really care about me. You just want to get off this island. That's all you want."

"A year ago, that was true," Cole said. "But not anymore."

"You haven't changed," Peter challenged, his voice growing louder. "You would beat me up again if you had the chance."

Cole shook his head. "I could beat you up right now, but I won't."

"You won't, 'cause you're scared of Garvey," Peter said. "And 'cause you're scared of jail."

Again Cole shook his head. "It's because I've had a lot of time to think. And besides, if you thought I might beat you up again, why did you tell Garvey you wanted to come alone with me this morning?"

Peter bent down, pretending to tie his boot.

"You have to believe me," Cole pleaded. "I'll do anything to help you and make things right. It doesn't do any good to stay mad."

Suddenly Peter sprang up, shoving Cole hard, and sending him stumbling to the ground. "Stay away from me! I don't need your help!" he screamed.

"I'm so sorry," Cole repeated.

"You're not sorry for anything!" Peter shouted. He kicked at the ground, pelting Cole with gravel and dirt.

Shielding his face, Cole got to his feet, but

Peter stormed forward and shoved him again. "Why don't you beat me up again? I don't care anymore!"

Cole quietly stood his ground.

"Maybe you're scared of me," Peter said, swinging his fists. He struck Cole squarely in the face. "Go ahead, hit me!" he taunted. "Kill me. I don't care anymore."

"You do care," Cole said, shielding his face. "I'm not ever going to hurt you again. Can't you see that?"

"Liar!" shouted Peter. He hit Cole hard in the gut. "You're scared of me."

When Cole refused to fight back, Peter grew bolder. Again and again he struck Cole with his bare fists. Cole raised his arms to try to ward off the blows, but he didn't fight back, nor did he run. This only made Peter angrier. He hit harder.

As the blows pummeled him, Cole's own anger smoldered. He grabbed deep breaths. He would not get angry. Not now. As he tried to back away, he stumbled and fell. Peter was on him instantly, hitting and yelling. All Cole could do was curl his knees up to his chest and try to cover his face.

Then Peter started kicking him. To Cole it felt as if a sledgehammer was striking his chest and arms. He rolled away, but the next kick caught him in the face and slammed his head back. He tasted blood. The world spun in lazy circles. The hammer kept hitting. "Stop!" Cole gasped. "Please stop!"

"Then fight, you coward!" Peter screamed like a madman.

"I'm not going to fight you," Cole shouted as the next angry kick to his stomach took his breath away. Then the kicking stopped. Cole opened his eyes in time to see Peter sink to his knees next to him, crying. Peter's body shook with great hiccuping sobs.

"Are you okay?" Cole asked, grimacing from his pain.

"I'm scared," cried Peter. "I'm so scared. My thinking gets all mixed up, and I feel like the whole world is falling on me."

Wincing, Cole sat up. "How can I make you believe that you don't ever have to be scared of me again?"

"You just say that," Peter sobbed.

"Peter, I'm not a bad person. I got mad at you 'cause I was really mad at myself. I thought my dad beat me because I was worthless." Cole paused. "The dances, carving the totem, carrying the ancestor rock, touching the Spirit Bear, it was all the same thing—it was finding out who I really was."

"You're a jerk," Peter sobbed. "That's what you are."

Cole fought back his own tears. "I'm part of some big circle that I don't understand. And so are you. Life, death, good and bad, everything is part of that circle. When I hurt you, I hurt myself, too. I don't think I'll ever heal from what I did to you, but I'm sorry, Peter. I really am sorry."

Peter knelt, crying, his body bent forward. Cole, not knowing what else to do, wrapped his arms around Peter's shoulders. For a long time, Peter let himself be hugged, leaning back into Cole.

And that was when it appeared. Not twenty feet away, it stood watching them: the Spirit Bear.

"Look," Cole whispered, letting go of Peter.

Peter still sniffled, staring down at the ground.

"Look," Cole whispered louder, nudging him. "It's the Spirit Bear."

Peter raised his head and stared, his mouth opened in amazement. "Will it hurt us?" he whispered.

"No," Cole whispered back. "We're not threatening it. You and I have both become invisible."

Peter looked at Cole, puzzled.

"Never mind, I'll explain later," Cole whispered.

For a full minute, the bear stood frozen in

place, gazing at them. The chattering of a squirrel nearby echoed like thunder in the silence. Then, as suddenly as it had appeared, the Spirit Bear swung its massive head around and ambled away, vanishing ghostlike into the trees.

Peter drew in a deep breath as if waking from a long sleep. "Did we really see what I think we just saw?"

Cole smiled and shrugged. "They say there aren't any Spirit Bears here."

"But I saw one," Peter insisted. "Will anyone believe us?"

"It doesn't matter what other people think or believe," Cole said. "It's what *you* believe. That's what's important."

That morning, as Cole and Peter soaked, a warm silence blanketed the pond. Afterward, they found a second ancestor rock so both could roll their anger down the slope. When they headed back to camp, Cole's face was swollen, and he hugged at his sore ribs with an elbow.

"Are you okay?" Peter asked.

Cole licked at his numb and swollen lips, and grimaced. Still, he smiled. "I'd hate to go through that again."

Peter walked without speaking.

When they arrived back in camp, Cole broke

the silence. Standing beside the totems, he explained to Peter that being invisible was being a part of life's circle and accepting it. "This morning, when we forgave each other, we also forgave ourselves," he said. "We allowed ourselves to become a part of the big circle. That's why we saw the Spirit Bear."

"What makes you think I forgave you?" Peter said.

Cole pulled off the backpack. "I have something I want to give you," he said. He took out the folded at.óow. "Garvey gave this to me as a symbol of friendship and to show he trusted me." He handed the at.óow to Peter. "Now I want you to have it."

"Are you saying you trust me?" Peter asked.

Cole nodded. "I hope someday you'll trust me."

Peter stared at the at.óow as he spoke. "I want to help you carve the blank space on your totem, the space you saved for your dance of anger."

Cole hesitated. "Okay." He ran to the cabin and returned with the knives.

For the next two hours Cole and Peter carved together. When they finished, Cole hollered for Garvey to come from the cabin and take a look at the nearly perfect circle that now completed the totem.

When Garvey joined the boys, he stared down at the log and at what they had carved. "You carved a perfect circle," he said, a soft smile tugging at his lips. "Why a circle?"

Cole and Peter glanced nervously at each other, neither wanting to speak.

"Could it be because every part of a circle is both a beginning and an end?" Garvey asked. "And everything is one?"

Peter shrugged awkwardly and grinned at Cole. "A circle is all I could teach him to carve."

Cole smiled and nodded. "I'm a slow learner. But I'm working on it."

AUTHOR'S NOTE

Circle Justice has been practiced by native cultures for many centuries. Only recently has the concept been given a chance to work within some modern U.S. judicial systems. It may be argued that a beating victim would never be sent to an island to face his attacker, as is portrayed in this novel. The strength of Circle Justice, however, comes from the creativity of the individual members within each Healing Circle. I would hope that in real life, any healing path would remain a possibility.

Spirit Bears actually do exist off the coast of British Columbia. I have refrained from describing exactly where they are, in an attempt to preserve their threatened privacy and habitat. During the research for this book, however, a three-hundred-pound male Spirit Bear actually approached to within twenty feet of where I stood. It was indeed a magnificent sight, one worth preserving for future generations.

TOUCHING
SPIRIT
BEAR

BEN MIKAELSEN

DISCUSSION QUESTIONS

1. Why was Cole such an angry person?

2. Cole thinks his parents hate him. How do you think he feels about himself? Why?

3. Edwin tells Cole that "anger keeps you lost." What does he mean?

4. When Edwin takes Cole to the island for the first time, Cole asks him, "What is there to learn?" What do you think Edwin felt Cole could learn from being alone on the island?

5. When Cole first encounters the Spirit Bear he reacts with malice. What is it that changes Cole's attitude and makes him wish that the Spirit Bear would reappear?

6. Being mauled by the Spirit Bear and facing

death seems to change Cole for the better. Why do you think this horrific experience has such a positive effect on him?

7. Edwin forces Cole to soak in freezing cold water and carry the ancestor rock up the hill. What does Cole learn from doing what Edwin asks of him? Can you think of a time when you benefited from something you did against your will?

8. To most people, Cole seems beyond hope. Why do Edwin and Garvey make such a personal investment in Cole's future?

9. Cole's attack leaves Peter with permanent physical damage and deep psychological damage. Do you think Peter should forgive Cole? Why?

10. How does Native American Circle Justice help save Cole's life?

11. With Circle Justice, everything in life is connected. How do the actions of other characters in the book connect to Cole's crime and his eventual healing?

12. The Circle Justice system works for Cole and

allows him to reach a place of healing, eventually enabling him to help Peter as well. How might the outcome of Cole's story have been different if he'd gone to prison?

INTERVIEW QUESTIONS

1. What inspired you to write *Touching Spirit Bear*?

The idea for *Touching Spirit Bear* came from different directions. My own past was one of being an at-risk student, raised in a foreign country, never schooled in any way until fourth grade. And then I was away at a boarding school with strict English matrons who would strap my hand with leather straps for something done wrong. I've also raised a black bear named Buffy, and noticing how Buffy mirrors my own moods gave me the idea for the Spirit Bear mirroring Cole's attitudes. I even had a real Spirit Bear walk up to within twenty feet of me on a shoreline once. What a magnificent sight. I met a native spiritual leader in British Columbia who taught me how he worked with juveniles in his villages. My research took me up to both British Columbia and Alaska, where real banishments took place. Also, a friend of mine who works as a lawyer with traditional justice in Minneapolis introduced me to Circle Justice, more commonly known as Restorative Justice. All of these ingredients helped to define the final book. The main catalyst for the book though was the morning I turned on the television and watched the tragedy of Columbine play out in front of my eyes.

2. Are any of the characters or events in *Touching Spirit Bear* based on actual people or your personal experiences?

The characters are both fictitious and real. I came from a very dysfunctional family, which set the stage for Cole having such a family. The characters Peter, Cole, Garvey, and Edwin all mirror who I was at different times in my life. I didn't have to imagine Cole's anger or Peter's feeling of helplessness one bit to portray them. But I also know there were many lessons I learned when I discovered that life could be wonderful if we treat it so. Those lessons I portrayed with Garvey and Edwin.

3. What do you see as the most valuable lesson Cole learns from his experience on the island?

The most valuable lesson Cole learns on the island is that he is a part of life's circle. And what that means is that everything in his life and everything he does is connected. He can't hurt anything without hurting himself. When Cole realizes that he has been a fool thinking he controlled his life, that day he surrenders to life and allows himself to be part of the circle. He realizes that controlling life and making good decisions that affect life are two different things. He can make decisions that positively mold his life and at the same time realize that he is a part of a larger current of life that controls all people and all things.

4. Do you think Cole would have had less of a chance to change for the better if he'd gone to jail instead of participating in Circle Justice?

If Cole had been sent to jail, he would most likely have been housed with kids who shared his negative attitude. I can't imagine what other influence besides isolation could have made him search into his soul the way he did on the island. Jail would have served to simply punish Cole. Perhaps fear of future punishment would have changed his future behavior, but I don't think it would have changed his heart the way being on the island did.

5. Could you survive a year alone on the island Cole is banished to?

Yes, I truly do think I could undergo such an experience. Many events in my life have served to separate me from society for long periods of introspection. I've gone up to boundary waters in Northern Minnesota on a couple of occasions for extended periods alone in the woods. Also, in 1976, I rode a horse across the United States from Northern Minnesota to Oregon. The months I spent, mostly alone, during that ride were times when I struggled with my anger the way Cole did on the island. For the last twenty-five years I have lived in a log home away from people in the mountains of Montana. Seclusion has never been difficult for me. What has been difficult is coming to the realization that I'm a good person, and that if I can get over my anger, life can be the most wonderful experience ever imagined.

6. Edwin introduces some rituals meant to help Cole deal with his anger. Do any of your own strategies for coping with anger resemble Edwin's?

The rituals Edwin shows to Cole are not magic or something only he could communicate. They are simply devices that allowed Cole to look inward. The cold pond took Cole's mind off his anger long enough to reflect objectively on that anger. Carrying the ancestor rock was a struggle that made him focus on the rock so that his mind did not wander away from the words Edwin spoke as they climbed. Breaking the sticks of anger, rolling away his anger with the rock, dancing the dances, and carving the totems, these were all devices that allowed Cole to focus inward. In my own life I have found many methods that may not be the same as Cole's experience, but they have served the same purpose. For me, starting each day with quiet time is important. Taking time whenever I can to walk in the woods and to reflect on how I am a part of all that is around me—I find that very helpful. I love the notion that reality is not what happens around me but how I react to what happens. If a truck drives past me, that is not reality. If I step in front of that truck, I choose to create one reality. If I choose to step out of its way, that creates another reality. All people, especially young people, need to know the power they carry to affect their own reality.

7. When you are developing a character that goes through the kind of grueling emotional ride that Cole experiences, how does it affect you?

For me, developing the character of Cole was to revisit my own past. This was not comfortable. It meant dredging up emotions and feelings that I thought were comfortably settled in my own past. It was very uncomfortable to revisit that anger and fear, but it was necessary to communicate the raw anger that Cole felt at the beginning of *Touching Spirit Bear*.

8. What do you find to be the most challenging and the most gratifying aspects of being an author?

The most challenging aspect of being an author is that nothing really prepares you for the journey. Each book, each contract, each appearance, is a fresh challenge and uncharted territory. It has been a most wonderful journey that has demanded that I believe totally in myself. Nobody is there to hold your hand at two A.M. when you are on the thirteenth rewrite and a chapter isn't working. Sometimes, after six months of working on a book, you find yourself doubting the very premise of your novel. At those times, being a successful author demands that you dig way deep inside of yourself and believe in that self. As for the most rewarding aspect, that would have to be seeing the completed book and experiencing how it affects life. To have a child come up and tell you that your book was the first book they ever read and that now they want to read more, what could be more satisfying than that? I am able to travel now to pretty much anywhere I want and meet the most wonderful people I could ever have imagined. Life has become stir-fried, but is so delicious!

9. You obviously have a deep respect for nature and the lessons it can teach us. Where do you think that deep respect comes from?

I would have to say my respect for nature comes from two places. Because I grew up without many friends, I spent most of my time alone. I grew to love animals because they didn't beat me up or tease me. I learned to love the unconditional love that animals offered. I also came to love nature from my travels. To stand on the great plains of the Maasai Mara in Kenya and to see a herd of elephants in one direction, and to turn your head slowly and see giraffes, hippopotamuses, lions, and zebras as far as the eye can see, that makes me realize how important it is to protect our planet. If the only place we can see these magnificent animals is in a zoo, it is our own humanity that we have caged. My many years of being alone in nature have allowed me to listen to and watch the life cycles evolving around me. We have so much to learn from the earth and her creatures. She is our greatest teacher if we only listen.

10. How did Buffy, the black bear you adopted and raised, come to be a part of your family?

Buffy was a research animal. I don't know a whole lot about his past, except that he had been declawed at a research facility and would most likely have been killed. Once they declaw an animal it cannot be released into the wild and zoos no longer want them for display. I have the same federal and state licenses as a zoo, which allows me to raise Buffy. But I do not recommend that people raise wild animals. I've seen many, many cases where people have tried and it always ends up tragically for the animal. If you raise a 50-pound dog wrongly, it becomes a 50-pound nuisance. If you raise a 750-pound bear wrongly, it can kill you. Raising Buffy has been a rewarding experience for me only because I have devoted my life to his care and well-being.

11. Have you learned things from Buffy, as Cole learned things from the Spirit Bear?

Yes, I have learned so many things from Buffy—the same lessons that Cole learned from the Spirit Bear. Buffy has taught me that how I treat him is how he treats me. This is also so true of how we treat the world in which we live. Buffy also taught me to be sensitive and kind. The only way Buffy will trust me is if I am trustworthy. You can't lie to a bear the way you can to a human. Buffy has also taught me to accept and to forgive myself.

Also by Ben Mikaelsen

Hc 0-06-009004-9
Pb 0-06-009006-5

Hc 0-380-97745-1
Pb 0-380-80561-8

TREE GIRL is a chilling and inspiring tale of a fifteen-year-old Guatemalan girl who witnesses the horrors of guerrilla warfare from the safety of a tree and vows never to climb again.

≣HarperTempest
An Imprint of HarperCollinsPublishers

RED MIDNIGHT follows Santiago and his frightened little sister on a heart-pounding voyage to America in a treacherously small kayak. Along the way, storms and the threat of pirates test their courage in this gripping survival story.

≣HarperTrophy®
An Imprint of HarperCollinsPublishers

≣HarperCollins*Children'sBooks*

An Imprint of HarperCollinsPublishers

www.harperchildrens.com • www.harpertempest.com
www.benmikaelsen.com